PRAISE FOR *WILD RIVER*:

An Amazon Best Book of the Month
A Junior Library Guild Selection

"Newbery Honoree Philbrick twines a heartfelt message about teamwork and forgiveness with realistic dangers in this **page-turning survival story. A battle for power keeps the** tension high, as do plenty of twists and cliffhangers." —*Publishers Weekly*

"As he did with *Wildfire,* Newbery Honoree Philbrick has crafted another action tale for young readers that's impossible to put down. **Readers will need to strap on their helmets and prepare for a wild ride.**" —*Kirkus Reviews*

PRAISE FOR *WILDFIRE*:

★ "**An intense tale of survival and action**. A must-have for all upper elementary/middle grade libraries."
—*School Library Journal*, starred review

★ "Short chapters, outstanding cover art, and a breathless pace make this a fine choice for reluctant readers. **Outstanding suspense**." —*Kirkus Reviews*, starred review

★ "**Action lovers will relish every word**. With *Wildfire*—reminiscent of *Hatchet* and the real-life saga *Lost on a Mountain in Maine*—Philbrick transforms a raging inferno into an impressively plotted escape story full of heart and soul."
—*BookPage*, starred review

WILD RIVER

ALSO BY RODMAN PHILBRICK

Wildfire

Freak the Mighty

Max the Mighty

The Fire Pony

REM World

The Last Book in the Universe

The Young Man and the Sea

The Mostly True Adventures of Homer P. Figg

Zane and the Hurricane: A Story of Katrina

The Big Dark

Who Killed Darius Drake?: A Mystery

*Stay Alive: The Journal of Douglas Allen Deeds,
The Donner Party Expedition, 1846*

WILD RIVER

A NOVEL

Rodman Philbrick

Scholastic Inc.

Copyright © 2021 by Rodman Philbrick

This book was originally published in hardcover by Scholastic Press in 2021.

All rights reserved. Published by Scholastic Inc., *Publishers since 1920*. SCHOLASTIC and associated logos are trademarks and/or registered trademarks of Scholastic Inc.

ISBN 978-1-338-64729-7

10 9 8 7 6 5 4 3 2 1   22 23 24 25 26

Printed in the U.S.A.   40

This edition first printing 2022

Book design by Nina Goffi

For Jan Bamberger, who suggested a
white-water adventure and kept
guiding it down the river

Prologue

The blamers and the shamers have it all wrong about the horrible events at Crazy River. Nobody knew what was going to happen, so it's nobody's fault. A free trip to Montana to experience a white-water rafting adventure? Who could say no to that? Not me, for sure. And not any of the other kids in Project Future Leaders. Which was some kind of joke, or I wouldn't have been selected to participate. Because, believe me, nobody looks at me and says, "Now, there's a born leader!" They see Daniel Redmayne, a pale, skinny kid with glasses and a lucky Red Sox cap. A middle schooler who would rather write a fantasy story or draw a cartoon than do his homework. A student who teachers say needs motivation, and often fails to participate in class. *Lost in his own world*, one of them wrote on my last report card. So, not a likely pick for anything.

Maybe the others were more qualified, and I was just a mistake. Or that's what I thought at the time. Whatever, there were five of us in the van that day, heading for a river somewhere deep in the Montana wilderness. Me,

Deke, Tony, Mia, and the quiet girl with the bouncy dreads, Imani. Plus two adult supervisors, or "guards," as Deke liked to joke. Yuk, yuk. And no matter how unfunny, you have to laugh at Deke's jokes or he'll pound you. Sky Hanson, the rafting guide, was driving. Cindi Beacon— yes, *that* Cindi Beacon—was there for supervision and inspiration. As you probably already know, she was the top striker for the US national team that won the last World Cup, and for sure the most famous person any of us had ever met. I know girls who have her poster on their walls. Boys, too.

Expensive people, expensive trip. Good thing it was sponsored by Byron James, the famous billionaire inventor. What was he thinking? Probably that our new regional middle school was being named for him, and this was his way of saying thanks.

Big mistake, as it turned out. Huge. But he had no way of knowing how it would turn out, or how many of us would die.

Day One

1.

Crazy River, Here We Come

I t starts out as the best day ever. For a kid from a small town in New Hampshire, Montana is freaking awesome. The place has mountains high enough to scratch the pure blue sky, ranches half as big as the entire state of Rhode Island, and grizzly bears and mountain lions and herds of wild buffalo. And the best part? They still have real live, actual cowboys. I mean, think about it!

Deke pretends to be bored, but most of us kids are staring out the van windows like we can't believe our eyes. Our white-water guide, a really friendly dude with a bushy blond beard and a matching ponytail, has been pointing out the sights. Mostly mountains and canyons with strange names, and glints of creeks and rivers way down in the steep ravines.

"Couple more miles," he says cheerfully. "Sorry our primary destination didn't work out, but the Crazy, you have my word it will deliver the goods."

Crazy is the name of the river we're heading for, and we've got our fingers crossed that it won't be as low and dry as the first choice. Can't have a white-water adventure without white-water rapids, right? So it's worth driving a hundred miles farther into the wilderness for what Sky promises will be "the rafting ride of a lifetime."

Strapped into a seat in the third row, Mia raises her hand and waits until one of the grown-ups spots it in the rearview. "Yes?"

"When do we eat?"

Sky shakes his head and chuckles. "Girl, you must have a hollow leg. We had a big breakfast, and you had a big lunch. Two helpings of ice cream, as I recall. To answer your question, next meal will be over a campfire on a sandy beach. Until then, you'll find snacks in the blue cooler."

Mia makes an impish face. I doubt she's really hungry. Just making herself known. Deke gives her a sullen look. She crosses her arms and ignores him. Tony sleeps with his head leaning against the window, oblivious as usual. And our famous soccer player, Cindi Beacon, the one they call Tiny Dancer because of her size and her moves, is playing a game on her phone. No cell reception out in the wilderness, or she'd probably be reporting back to her agent, which she does a lot. From what I can tell, it's pretty complicated being a celebrity. Still, she's really nice and down-to-earth, and doesn't brag about being famous.

The van turns onto an even smaller road, more like a rutted trail. We left the pavement long ago, but this is a lot bouncier.

"Over there!" We strain to see where Sky is pointing. "Through those trees. Big Medicine Dam, one of the oldest in the state. Built for purposes of irrigation, and retrofitted for flow control in the 1950s. Some want to tear it down and free the river. Others think it needs to be rebuilt for safety. All we care is that it feeds the Crazy."

The van comes to a stop, seemingly at no place in particular, surrounded by forest.

Once we're all out, Sky claps his hands together. "We'll hike down from here. Cindi and I will portage the raft. Everybody else, take a pack. And while you're strapping up, we'll give the sat phone another try."

Sky and Cindi bend over the satellite phone, punching buttons and shaking their heads in frustration. After a brief discussion, they nod in agreement.

Sky strides back to us, clearing his throat. "Listen up, people! We had to make a decision. Base was duly notified about abandoning our first destination. But the phone is still down—looks like the battery croaked—so we can't contact them to let them know the Crazy is our final choice, understood? It's not as if we'll be alone on the river. Bound to cross paths with other tour groups, who are likely to have a working sat phone. In light of that, we have decided to proceed with our plan to raft the Crazy, and make contact later."

We all cheer, even Deke. Crazy River, here we come.

2.

Why They Call It Crazy

The hike down to the riverbed would be tough even without the packs. The trail is steep and twisty and the big pack feels like I'm top-heavy, and if I'm not careful, I'll tip over backward. I'm not the only one. Imani really does fall over, and when Deke laughs and makes fun of her, Sky makes him take her pack, too.

"This is a team effort," he says, very firm. "One of us falls, we pick our teammate up. Do whatever is necessary to preserve the team. Understood?"

Deke smirks but agrees. Sky is really nice and everything, but you get the idea it wouldn't be smart to make him mad. I'm worried that if Deke doesn't stop being such a jerk, he's going to ruin it for the rest of us.

When we finally get down to river level, there's a lot of work to do. Sky inflates the bright red raft and prepares it for launch. When it's ready, Cindi helps us stow and secure the packs, which contain all the food and gear we'll need for the three-day journey. Then she takes charge of making sure our bulky life jackets are adjusted and the chin straps on our helmets are fastened. I make sure the elastic strap on my glasses is tight.

Just before we climb into the raft, I finally get a chance to check out the scenery. Which is spectacular. There are high mountains all around us, with peaks like the points of a crown. Awesome. The clear mountain water, rushing around rocks and boulders, sounds like a distant crowd cheering. Across the river, tall fir trees line the water's edge like a row of dull green sentries. The ravine walls are higher and steeper than I expected, especially on the opposite shore. And it's just us. Not another raft in sight. Feels like we're all alone in the world. Us and the river and the unspoiled scenery. Not a bad feeling, and just scary enough to be exciting.

One by one, as our names are called, we pile into the big raft. Sky passes out paddles and shows us how to dip the blades and pull, but not too deep. "First rule of raft club, stay in the raft! Okay, for purposes of steering, you will be divided into two teams, left and right. Deke, Tony, and Cindi, you are Team Blue. Mia, Daniel, Imani, and me, we are Team Red. Got it? Today I'll be the raft commander and shout out directions. Okay? Everybody good? Here goes! Shove off!"

The current sweeps us away from shore, and the big raft starts spinning. Sky finally gets us pointed in the right direction by shouting "Red" or "Blue." At first I'm afraid to use my paddle—I really, really don't want to fall out of the raft—but then I start to get the hang of it. It's fun!

At the first turn, we're almost swept up onto the rocky shore. At the last moment, we manage to get the raft back into the middle of the river. "Well done!" Sky exclaims. "You're getting the hang of it. Two more turns and we'll find the rapids. Or they'll find us!"

He explains this is how the river got its name. So many crazy twists and turns.

We manage to keep the raft centered through both turns, and then, suddenly, we start to pick up speed, like we're sliding down a slippery ladder. Going faster and faster. I hear it before we see it, the roar of the white-water rapids.

A second later, the bottom of the world seems to drop away. Waves, spray, big rocks, they all blur together. I'm instantly soaked from head to foot, and that's fun, too. Like the coolest ride in the coolest water park ever. The raft bobs and tips, and a couple of times it almost flips over. Or that's what it feels like. I think most of us are screaming, partly in terror and partly for the sheer fun of it. And we're all improving with the paddle work. The only one not cheering is Imani, but from the way she handles her paddle, I'm guessing this isn't her first rafting experience.

Sky has his hands full keeping us upright. Suddenly we're spinning backward and it's all I can do to stay in the raft, let alone follow Sky's shouted instructions.

"RED RED RED!"

He's digging like mad with his own paddle. We're heading right for a huge white boulder, waves breaking all around it. I don't know what to do, or how to help. We're doomed for sure. But somehow Sky shoves us off, and then we're spinning the other way and I get a face full of water that makes it hard to see.

Next thing I know, we're out of the rapids and slowing down as the river widens. Our screams turn to cheers.

We made it!

And maybe if we'd stopped right there, all of us would have survived.

3.

The Luckiest Kid in the World

We make camp on a sandy beach, as promised, under yellow-tinted cliffs that put us in shadow long before the sun goes down. We unload the raft, drag it as far from the water as possible, and tie it to a scraggly tree. The place is beautiful in a slightly spooky way, the way the cliffs have been carved out of the sandstone ravine. It's so different from New Hampshire that we might as well be on Mars.

Sky calls the camp Tranquility Base. "First thing, set up our tents. Five tents in line with where the raft is tethered. Cindi will assist. While you're doing that, I'll get the campfire going."

After the tents are set up, Sky asks us to gather around the fire. "I understand that none of you really know each other. For the most part you attended different elementary schools, is that correct? Okay. I also gather that some of you are wondering how you got picked to participate in this program. It came out of the blue, right? A letter in the mail, offering you the chance to participate. All I know about the selection process is that you've been chosen because the Byron James Foundation thinks you might benefit from the experience. Clear?"

Some of us nod. Deke catches Tony's attention and rolls his eyes.

"Here's what we're going to do," Sky says. "Each of you will stand up in turn, state your name, and tell us a little something about yourselves. What you're interested in, what you do for fun, like that. Mia, if you don't mind, you go first."

She leaps to her feet with a big grin. Obviously, she doesn't mind at all. "I'm Maria Valentina Garcia, but I go by Mia, 'cause that's what my abuela calls me. My grandmother. My dad is a dentist, my mom runs the office. I have two little brothers. When I grow up, I'm gonna be a lawyer. Not the money kind, the kind that helps people. My favorite thing to do is read books." Pleased with herself, she plops to the sand and hugs her knees.

"Deke?"

He sighs, and stands reluctantly, both hands thrust into his pockets. Big for his age, and built like a linebacker, with blond hair close cut and light blue eyes that can be cruel or bored. "Is this like *Survivor* or something? Because that show is so lame."

We laugh because it's a little like *Survivor,* but without the cameras.

"State your name, please."

Another big sigh. "Okay, okay. Deacon Bailey. My mom

13

and dad work for Byron James, the zillionaire who's paying for all this, so that's probably why I got picked for the program. That and because I don't get straight As like my dad did when he was my age, and for some reason, he thinks this trip will help me do better." He snorts. "No chance!"

Most of the kids laugh, but it's a nervous laugh.

"My favorite thing is playing *Super Smash Brothers*. I'm really good at it, even if I'm not good at school." He shrugs like he couldn't care less what anybody thinks, and slumps down.

"Thanks, Deke. Tony? Tony? You're up."

"What?"

"Your turn."

"Oh yeah, sorry." He staggers to his feet, making a goony face, his nose and cheeks red with sunburn. "Anthony Meeks. Tony. My parents are just normal parents, which means they can be a pain." Our laughter encourages him, and he starts clowning around. "My favorite thing? I dunno, lots of things. *Candy Crush.* Firecrackers. Telling dumb jokes. Riding my trail bike. Hip-hop! Girls!"

"Thank you, Tony."

"Mortal Kombat!"

"Daniel."

I've been dreading this. Giving a talk in front of the class is, like, my worst nightmare. But at least I didn't have to study or memorize. And if this is the price of a white-water rafting adventure, so be it.

14

"Daniel Redmayne. Sorry, but I'm pretty boring. I have three little brothers and we share the same room, so earbuds are essential. This is the coolest thing I've ever done. I mean the raft, not me talking. Thank you."

"Thank you, Daniel. Imani?"

Imani is African American, with braids pulled into a ponytail and big brown eyes that for some reason look cautious. "Imani Walker," she says, without getting up. "I had fun today. Sorry, but I don't feel like talking. Maybe later."

Sky says, "That's okay. Whenever you're ready."

Something makes me think Imani has secrets like I've got secrets, but what hers are, exactly, I have no idea.

Which is sort of the opposite of Tony. He's just out there, being his silly self and wanting to make friends. He grins at me. "Dude, what did one toilet say to the other? You look a bit flushed!"

"Ha. Good one."

"Nah, it's stupid, but I like stupid jokes. Does that make me stupid?"

"No, it makes you funny."

"Thanks, dude! Cool. We're here to have fun, right? Like numerous adventures and stuff. Death-defying feats."

If we'd known how right he was about death-defying feats, we'd have bailed right then.

Supper is hot dogs on sticks toasted over the fire, and corn on the cob cooked in aluminum foil, and baked new potatoes that taste amazing with salt and pepper. Dessert is

15

little cups of half-melted ice cream from Sky's backpack cooler. Nobody complains, not even Deke, and we eat till our stomachs are bursting.

After, Sky tells a funny story about his first time camping out, and all the mistakes he made. Then he talks about what to expect on the river tomorrow. Cindi tells what it was like scoring the goal that won the big game, and how it was all instinct and muscle memory. By then we're all yawning and Sky calls it a night, and warns us we'll be up at first light.

"We may get some rain," he says. "Looks like a weather system is coming in from the west. If need be, I'll break out rain gear in the morning."

The way it works out, with five tents for seven people, I get a tent to myself. Which is a huge improvement on double bunk beds, and little brothers who have fart contests on a regular basis.

Lying there in my new sleeping bag, listening to the splashy murmur of the river, I figure I'm the luckiest kid in the world.

I fall asleep dreaming that Dad is taking his medication and acting normal, and there's nothing to be worried about anymore. What wakes me is rain pounding the tent, and the ground shaking, and a thundering roar in the distance, coming closer, and Sky Hanson screaming our names.

16

Day Two

4.

Gone, Gone, Gone

I jam my baseball cap on my head and stumble out of my tent into the crazy dark. Scared to death because I don't know what's happening, or why the adults are so frightened. Instantly the rain drenches through my clothes, right to my skin.

"The dam has failed!" Sky screams. "Flood! Flood! Get to higher ground! The cliffs!"

All I can see are shapes moving, so I follow them, my heart pounding like an insane drum.

Out of the darkness somebody grabs my hand. Somebody strong.

Sky shouts, "Got you, son! Climb, boy, climb! Quick as you can! Flood is coming!"

He lifts me up, shoves me against the cliff, and keeps me there until I find a foothold on the slippery rock. Some sort of instinct must be taking over, because without really knowing how, I'm scrambling up the cliff. Sky keeps shoving me from behind, pushing to lift me higher, guiding me to footholds.

I keep climbing, clinging like a magnet to the sandstone and using my fingertips to find the next handhold, because for sure I can't see. When I get as high as he can reach, Sky stops pushing and shouts for Tony. I know that others are scrambling up the cliff, kids I think, but I can't be sure. Panic is making me dizzy, and I'm terrified of falling, because the thunderous roar has turned into something else. Something far more terrifying. A continuous explosion that drowns out all of our screaming.

My hands find a ledge, and I pull myself over. There's room enough to stand up, but I stay flat, afraid of losing my balance. Looking over the edge, blinking against the rain, I see dark shapes getting closer. Kids being shoved up to the ledge by the adults below. Tony makes it, his eyes bugging out with fear. I reach over, grab an outstretched hand, and drag Mia up onto the ledge. She's shouting something, but I can't hear her. All I can hear is the roar coming down the ravine, closer and closer. Rushing water, yes, but other sounds. Snapping and breaking and pounding, loud enough to shake the ground, and the cliff itself.

Deke is shoved up and climbs right over me, finding a place on the ledge.

Right about then, a strange thing happens. Clouds roll away, revealing the moon, and suddenly I can make out Imani, just below me, and Cindi Beacon shoving her up the cliff, onto the ledge. Cindi with a look on her face so determined and so terrified that it almost stops my heart.

20

She knows she's going to die. She knows, but she's still doing her best to save Imani. It makes me want to reach down and touch her hand and say "thank you thank you," but I never get the chance. The shrieking roar gets louder and louder, and then it comes around the last bend in the river, exploding into the moonlight, and an enormous wave of broken trees and rolling boulders surges right up to the lip of the ledge, pounding at the cliff, threatening to snatch us away.

I close my eyes, expecting to die.

A million years go by. Several very long minutes for sure. Somehow, I'm still here, clinging to the ledge, and the roar is gradually subsiding. I sneak a peek over the edge.

The flood is at least ten feet below us now, and dropping. Cindi Beacon is nowhere to be seen. She's gone.

They're both gone, Sky and Cindi.

We're alone.

5.

What About Us?

Hard to tell when the sun comes up, because it never stops raining. Cool, constant rain, from clouds so low they seem just above the trees. In the pale gray light, I make out five of us perched on the ledge. Me, Deke, Tony, Mia, and Imani. All of us drenched and miserable.

"We shouldn't even be on this freakin' river," Deke complains. "The coaches were idiots."

Mia looks like she'd like to shove him off the ledge, even though he's twice her size. "Shut up, Deke. They saved our lives! And now they're dead!"

"It's their own fault." Deke folds his arms, defiant. He's the only one not shivering, like he has his own furnace of anger keeping him warm. "They changed rivers and never let anybody know. That's, like, super against the rules."

"Be quiet and let me think," Mia says fiercely. "We have to find a way off this ledge or we'll be dead, too."

"Maybe you," Deke says. "I'll be just fine."

"Can we stop fighting?" I suggest. "I, um, think Mia's

right. We could die of exposure. We need to get out of the rain, warm up somehow."

Mia stands up, leaning back against the sandstone cliff to keep her balance. "It's not that." She points down at the inside of the ledge. "It's that! See that crack? An hour ago, it was barely wider than my thumb. I think the flood weakened the wall, and if that crack gets any wider, this ledge will fall off the cliff."

Suddenly, Deke looks as scared as the rest of us. But not so scared he doesn't have an idea. He cranes his head, studying the cliff above. "Only way off is up," he says. "Tony, give me a boost."

Goofy, funny Tony had been trying to make friends with Deke since we first met at the airport, so he's eager to help, lacing his fingers together and giving Deke a boost up to a ledge so narrow he has to turn his feet sideways. Maybe five inches of sandstone, barely enough for a foothold.

Scary. But Deke makes it look easy, sliding along and gradually working his way upward until, ten feet above, he pulls himself up and over the cliff.

"Hey! What about us?"

His sneering face appears over the edge. "Better get climbing, you losers. Didn't you hear what Miss Know-It-All said? Your little world is about to end."

He's not wrong. The crack in the ledge is getting bigger, no doubt about it.

6.

The Next Thing

It's tricky getting all of us up to the top of the ravine, one by one. We have no choice but to pitch in and help each other. Even Deke does his part, using his strength to pull us over. Of course, he keeps running his mouth and making fun of whoever happens to be in his sights. "Imani, what kind of name is that? You an illegal, is that why you don't have much to say?" She shakes her head, disgusted.

Deke has a thing about names, apparently, because he makes fun of mine, too. "Daniel the spaniel, all bark and no bite," he says, pulling me up over the edge.

"Leave him alone," Mia says. "He was the last one up. That took courage."

"Who made you the boss?" he says with a sneer.

"Yeah, who?" Tony chimes in.

"I'm going to find shelter," Mia announces firmly. "Follow or not, your choice."

She hefts the backpack and marches along a path a few yards back from the edge of the cliff. Sky had tossed the pack up to her on the ledge. It was one of the last things he did. I follow, wondering what's in the pack. Clothing? Food? If it's something good, will she share?

I'm starving, that's my excuse for having such selfish thoughts.

Looking over the cliff edge gives me a bird's-eye view of the flood destruction. The riverbed, so clear and perfect on our raft trip, is piled high with broken trees and boulders. So we can't raft our way out of this even if we had a raft, which we don't. Our camping area lies buried under twenty feet of wreckage.

The only gear that survived is the backpack Sky handed up to Mia. The pack that maybe has emergency rations. I'm following that as much as I'm following her. So is Imani, a few yards behind me on the path.

The next thing makes me forget all about food. A very loud *crack!* that sounds like an echoing rifle shot, only deeper. And a weird shifting under my feet.

"RUN!" I scream.

Mia has already veered from the path and is sprinting into the trees, away from the cliff.

We've barely had enough time to catch our breath, and once again we're running for our lives. It's not just the ledge that was damaged by the flood. A whole, massive section of the sandstone cliff is collapsing. And if we can't get away, can't get deep enough into the woods, we'll plummet into the wreckage of the river below.

"RUN!"

7.

Staying Alive

I'm running so fast it feels almost like flying, my feet barely touching the ground. Or maybe that's the ground dropping out from under me, which is so terrifying a thought that I run even faster. Desperate to get ahead of that sickening rumble of the cliff falling away. Raindrops blurring my glasses. Flashes of trees and leaves and Mia a few yards ahead of me, racing for her life, pack bobbing higher than her head.

I don't dare look back to see if the others are following us away from the ravine edge. Looking back might make me stop to help, and stopping means you die. And I'm so scared I can't think about anything but staying alive.

Don't die, don't die, don't die. The words on loop, screaming in my brain.

The rumble of the collapsing cliff fades away. In the silence that follows, all I can hear is my heart pounding. I made it. I'm alive. And then, with my glasses blurred, I run straight into a tree.

Wham, flat on my back.

Behind me, Deke hoots and laughs. "Oh, dude, that was perfect! Like a cartoon, the way you bounced backward!"

Not "Are you okay?" or offering to help me up.

I roll over, panting and wheezing and spitting out rainwater. Can't even respond to the big jerk because the breath has been knocked out of me.

I try to dry my glasses, but it's hopeless. Doesn't matter. We're lucky to be alive, all five of us.

Mia calls out, "Over here! Give me a hand, you guys!"

Staggering to my feet, I follow her voice. There she is, struggling with a blue tarp taken from the pack. She never quits, Mia. Always thinking ahead, doing what needs to be done.

She tosses me a bundle of rope. "You've got a jackknife, right? Cut off some lengths and we'll tie this to the tree branches. I swear if I don't get out of this stupid rain I'm going to melt."

Luckily the jackknife is buried deep in my pocket. A present from my dad, who said it might come in handy. If only he knew! I saw away, cutting the rope into shorter lengths.

Imani appears and silently takes some of the cut rope. With shaky hands, we tie one side of the blue tarp to some branches, up as high as we can reach. The other side we fasten to a couple of saplings, about waist high. The tarp slanting down so the rain runs off. We duck under the tarp, and Mia is grinning at us, me and Imani.

"We've got a roof over our heads!" she announces.

"Very cool. That was smart." I dry my glasses as best I can and peer out from the shelter. "Hey, Deke! Tony! Over here!"

Mia snorts. "Who says they're invited?"

"Sky Hanson," I remind her. "All for one and one for all."

"I guess," she says grudgingly.

Deke ducks under the tarp and joins us, followed eagerly by Tony. Who immediately rubs his hands together and wants to know what's for breakfast. Deke picks up on that and demands to know what's in the backpack. "I bet there's trail mix. Here, let me look."

Mia snatches it out of reach. "I'll share whatever there is, but this is my responsibility. Okay?"

"Not okay. Are you serious? But go ahead and check it out, we're all starving."

She carefully reopens the chunky backpack and rummages around.

"Any bacon?" Tony asks, making it a joke for Deke's approval.

Mia ignores him. There's a lot of useful stuff stowed in the pack. A flashlight, a compass, a fire-starter kit, a large clasp knife. Six metal cups for collecting and drinking rainwater. A space blanket, a first aid kit, and a lightweight one-quart pan for boiling water.

Mia hands each of us a cup. "See the lanyard? Clip it to your belts so you don't lose it."

28

"No food? Come on!"

Mia gives us a sly grin and lifts a large, obviously heavy package out of the backpack.

"Not bacon," she says. "Freeze-dried meals. Six servings per package."

"Let me see that," Deke demands, reaching out.

Mia shakes her head and is about to say something, when the sky cracks open.

8.

One Word

The lightning must have struck close by. A blinding flash and a blast of thunder so loud, so awesomely huge, that it feels like a punch to the chest. A reminder that even though I've been scared for hours, it can always get worse. That just because we survived a massive flood and a collapsing cliff doesn't mean we can't get struck by lightning.

One thing I've learned, long before this trip, is that something bad can happen at any moment. And you never know what it might be. As if to prove me right, a gust of wind rips the blue tarp from the saplings and sets it flapping like some crazy bird.

We're instantly drenched. The rain is coming down so hard I can barely see, but I'm pretty sure Mia is shoving stuff into the backpack as she shouts, "Grab the ropes! Grab the ropes!"

Easier said than done. The ropes are whipping around like skinny white snakes, but I finally manage to keep hold of one, and Deke has the other. He's laughing like he thinks this is fun. Not me. I feel like we're fighting for our lives, and there's nothing funny about that. But whatever, between us we get the tarp under control. And when the wind stops gusting, we tie the tarp to the saplings, and just like that, we have shelter again.

"That was excellent," Mia says to me and Deke. "Teamwork!"

"Yeah, right," Deke says dismissively. "What about the food? I'm starving."

"First things first," Mia says. "We need to make a fire so we can boil water."

"Why can't we just eat it out of the package?" Tony wants to know.

"Because you can't. I read the instructions, okay? We have to add two cups of boiling water to the package, let it sit for ten minutes, and then we'll have rice and beans with chicken."

Imani stands up. "The rain is starting to taper off. I'll look for dry leaves and firewood."

It's kind of shocking, because those are her first words since the flood.

Mia smiles her approval. "You should all help Imani," she suggests. "I'll check out the fire-starting kit."

Deke snorts. "Who made you the boss? I mean, seriously, what makes you think you can tell me what to do?"

"I'm not telling, I'm asking. Don't help if you don't want to."

31

"I'm not helping, either!" Tony chimes in. "You're right on, Deke. Totally. Who made her boss? Nobody, that's who!"

I stand up. "This is stupid. I'm cold and I'm hungry. We all are. After we've had a hot meal, we can argue about who should be in charge."

At first, it's just me helping Imani search for dry firewood, but eventually Deke and Tony pitch in. And still it takes us hours, because everything is soaking wet, even though the rain has stopped for the time being. Eventually, Imani comes up with the idea of looking under overhanging rocks. Which sounds goofy, but it works, because the ground under some of the rocks is still dry, and we're able to gather pine needles and leaves and small twigs.

It takes forever before we have enough to try starting a fire. The hot meal that should have been breakfast or lunch is going to be supper, if we're lucky.

When we finally have enough kindling and wood, Mia opens the tin fire-starter kit. It contains a box of waterproof matches, a half dozen self-igniting fire-starter cubes, and a flint for striking sparks when the other stuff runs out.

Mia asks which method we should use. Deke responds by grabbing the matches. Five minutes later, we have a small but warming fire and two cups of rainwater boiling in the pan.

Waiting ten minutes for the freeze-dried meal to soak up the boiling water seems to take forever. My stomach is growling so loud it sounds like I swallowed a puppy. We don't have any plates, so we have to take turns spooning the rice, beans, and chicken chunks out of the pan.

In the normal world, I'd never share a spoon. But this is so far from normal that nobody complains, we're too busy wolfing down the food. Which tastes delicious, by the way, even if there's not really enough to make us feel full.

"Break out another package," Deke says, wiping his mouth with the back of his hand. "I'm just getting warmed up."

"No," says Mia, hugging the zipped-up backpack. "We need to ration."

"Are you insane? Give me that pack, you little jerk. Or else."

"No!"

No. One word. That's all it took to start a war.

9.

Freeze-Dried Maggots

In case I forgot to mention, Deke towers over Mia. She's on the small side, and he's taller than any of us. And anger seems to make him even bigger.

"You know what you are?" he says, jabbing his finger in her direction. "A bossy little know-it-all. Every class has a loser like you. But this isn't school! You can't run to the teacher, or complain to the principal. You're not in charge of anything! You're not in charge of me, and for sure you're not in charge of the food."

If Mia is scared, she doesn't show it. "Why is it that when boys are in charge they're heroes, but when a girl steps up she's bossy?"

"Because you are?" Tony says, taunting.

If Mia had laser beams for eyes, he'd be a puff of smoke. "Whatever," she says. "Here's the deal. There are only twelve freeze-dried packets, okay? Eleven now that we've eaten one. We don't know how long it will take them to find us. We have to ration. One meal a day."

Deke waves angrily at the cloud-blackened sky. "Soon

as this blows over, they'll send up helicopters. By this time tomorrow, we'll be heading home."

"I hope so, I really do. But we can't be sure about that. They don't even know what river we were rafting, remember? This one is a hundred miles from where they thought we were going."

"Not that far. No way."

"When we found the first river was dry, we drove for almost two hours, remember?"

"Just shut up. They'll find us! Now hand it over!"

"Coach Sky gave me the backpack. It was the last thing he did. He could have given it to you, but he gave it to me. So I'm responsible."

Deke clenches his fists. Is he going to hit Mia? If he does, I'll have to stop him. Or try my best. But a moment later, he starts chuckling, like everything he just said was meant to be a joke. "You know what? I think I lost my appetite. You can keep your stupid freeze-dried food. What flavor was it? Garbage pail? Toilet bowl?"

"That's disgusting," Imani says. "How come boys always have to be disgusting?"

"Because it's fun!" Tony is gleeful. "That wasn't rice, it was freeze-dried maggots!"

Even Mia laughs at that. Because it's true, maggots do look a bit like rice. Anyhow, all the bad jokes relieve the tension, but there's something in Deke's eyes that makes

35

me worry it isn't over. No way is he going to back down, or let anyone boss him around.

He's still trouble, I'm sure of it.

That's how we spend the first night after the flood, five of us jammed together under the tarp, trying to stay dry. We take turns using the space blanket because our little fire has gone out and none of us want to risk searching for dry kindling in the dark. Not with the ravine edge looming. The blanket helps a little, but isn't really necessary. It's not actually cold, it's just damp and miserable.

The choice is to sleep lying on the wet ground or sitting up. I choose sitting up, with my back against the tree the tarp is tied to. I keep nodding off, but not deep enough to be satisfying, restful sleep. It doesn't help that Tony is snoring like an outboard motor.

My brain is jagged with stuff to worry about. Things back home, mostly, which is weird because here we are, lost in the wilderness without enough to eat and no idea how to get back to civilization. But I can't help worrying about my dad, who has a mental illness. Bipolar disorder. Sometimes he gets these wild thoughts, like he has an idea that's going to change the world and he doesn't sleep for days. Then he crashes and just lies in bed and feels sad and depressed. Mostly his medication helps keep him on the level, but not always.

I hope me being missing doesn't freak him out or trigger an episode. Which makes it all the more important for us to find a way out of this situation, so I can let my family know I'm okay.

Deke may have a plan to make himself boss, but I've got a plan, too. Not to be the leader—I couldn't care less about that. A plan to stay alive. A plan to rescue ourselves.

Day Three

10.

Heigh-Ho for Elmer Fudd

As soon as Mia wakes up, I explain what I have in mind. Her eyes widen. "Great idea, Daniel! We'll discuss it after breakfast and make a decision."

I might be blushing. Not that anybody would notice. I'm pretty sure we're all too grimy and grumpy and hungry to pick up on that. Deke has an expression on his face that says *Don't even think about crossing me.* Tony looks scared and miserable. Imani isn't letting anything show, which she's really good at—lots of practice, I think. And Mia, she's as determined as ever, with a bright spark of energy in her large brown eyes.

"Good morning, everybody. Let's make breakfast!" She reaches into the pack. "Sorry, there's no actual breakfast meal. How about beef and noodles? That should be an energy boost, and we're going to need it."

Tony yawns and goes, "Huh? Say what?"

"Daniel, please explain your idea."

Now I really do feel embarrassed. Speaking out or

making suggestions is not my thing. But these are special circumstances, right?

I'm pretty sure my voice is shaking, at least at first. "Our mission was to raft down the Crazy River. From the drop-off point to the pickup location, the one Sky was going to phone in but never got the chance. The same location that other rafters would be using, if there are other rafters. Maybe there are, ahead of us. And if they survived, my guess is they'll be heading down-river. There's bound to be a road at the pickup location, because vans are supposed to be waiting for rafters, and a road means somebody will see us. So, what if our new mission is to follow the river to the pickup location? Better chance of rescue there than out here in the wilderness."

Tony looks puzzled, but Deke is nodding approval. "I like it, Danny boy. Instead of sitting around, hoping to be rescued, we take it into our own hands. I wonder how far it is from here?"

I shrug. "Not sure, but our trip was supposed to take three days, and from the way Sky talked about it, some of that was white water and a lot was paddling. I'm think-ing at least ten miles. Probably more. Maybe a lot more."

Everybody is for it. And that may be the only time that all five of us agreed on anything.

Collecting kindling and firewood goes quicker, because we've had practice and know not to waste time searching the wrong places. After breakfast, Mia carefully folds the blue tarp and repacks the backpack. Deke offers to carry it, and she declines.

"Your loss, girly whirl. Let me know if you change your mind."

Mia makes a face. She's sick of Deke's taunts, that much is obvious. When we're ready to get started, Mia says, "Follow me."

That gets a snickering laugh out of Tony. "Follow her right over a cliff, hey, Deke?"

"Shut up," Deke says.

Which shuts Tony up for the rest of the morning. Mia selects a path that's at least a hundred feet from the edge of the ravine and starts walking, briskly but carefully. None of us want to stumble and fall. We need to follow the path of the river, but not so close there's a danger of going over the edge, or causing another ledge to collapse.

An hour later, our hiking has turned into trudging. It's not fun shoving our way through prickly bushes and around piles of rock. Not in the misty rain, with our bellies already rumbling. In fact, it's downright miserable.

To lighten the mood, Mia starts singing. She has a nice voice, but the song is meant to be funny.

"Heigh-ho, heigh-ho, it's off to camp we go! In the rain and mud, like Elmer Fudd, heigh-ho, heigh-ho!"

43

Imani is the second to chime in. Ditto on the nice voice. Must be a girl thing, singing our way out of misery, because none of the boys join in. By the time they wear out the silly tune, we're well on our way. The scene of the disaster is behind us.

As to what lies ahead, I'm almost afraid to think about it.

11.

Boys Get More

It's hard to believe how much the river was wrecked by the flood, but there it is, right before our eyes. Masses of smashed trees piled high. Boulders as big as trucks, scattered like marbles. Shoals of glistening sand and mud, all of it strewn around like a giant had a temper tantrum and went nuts. Ripping away the grown-ups and leaving us kids on our own.

Must have been a zillion tons of water let loose when the dam broke, a force powerful enough to change the shape of the riverbed. Wiping out old curves and forming new ones.

We're taking a break, staring out over the edge of the ravine to the scene of destruction, when Mia says, "It wrecked the world, didn't it? Changed everything for the river, and for us."

Deke shrugs. "Proves my point. We shouldn't have been here."

Mia turns on him. "They didn't know what was going to happen!"

"Well, they should have. That was their job, keeping us safe."

"They tried. They died trying! It wasn't their fault. They were taking us on a cool adventure, teaching us leadership. They didn't know the dam was going to fail."

Deke has a mean-sounding laugh. "They found us an adventure, all right. Just because they're adults doesn't mean they didn't make a big mistake."

"Not on purpose! And they did keep us safe, in the end. We survived because of them."

"Believe what you want, girly whirl."

"Don't call me that!"

Deke grins, because he thinks he's winning. Poking her with cruel words, messing with her head.

"We should keep moving," I suggest.

Tony makes a dog-woofing noise and points at me. "Hey! Daniel the spaniel thinks he's the big man now! Deke, tell him who's the real boss!"

Deke ignores him. He wipes the rain off his dripping nose and strides to the path. Like if he's first in line, that makes him the leader. Which means he has to deal with the bristly bushes, and be the first to duck under snagging tree branches, and trip on roots hidden beneath damp leaves. At one point, he has a look like *What have I got myself into?* but he keeps on going. Mia second, then me and Imani, and Tony bringing up the rear. He doesn't look happy, probably because Deke has been as

46

snarky with him as he has been to the rest of us.

"How long is this going to take?" Tony wants to know, his voice almost breaking.

"As long as it takes!" Deke barks out from the front.

Mia shakes her head, but keeps her mouth shut. You can tell she's thinking, calculating the best way to handle the situation. If any of us are born leaders, it's her. Not because she's bossy—she's not—but because she thinks things through.

I wish Deke would see it her way, but that's never going to happen. It's all about him, and not about us, that's the difference.

Hard to know what time of day it is, with the clouds blocking out the sun, but Tony has a strap-on Disney wristwatch, so when he announces that it's noon, I believe him. "Twelve p.m. Lunchtime! I don't know about you guys, but I'm starving."

Mia ignores him, and keeps trudging along.

"Did you hear me? Time to stop for lunch. I'm hungry enough to eat a bowl of freeze-dried boogers!"

Everybody laughs, including Deke. It may be gross, but it's also funny. Especially if you've seen the ingredients before the boiled water gets poured over them.

"Sorry," Mia says. "Only ten meals left. We can't have three meals a day. One meal, that's it."

Deke stops striding and turns to face her. "You know what I heard? Girls have an extra layer of fat, so they can survive longer without food. So, it's only fair that the boys get more."

Mia ignores that, tries to get around him. He blocks her.

"What do you say, girly whirl? What does your extra layer of fat say?"

I shout, "Hey! Let her go!"

Deke gives me a long look. Finally, he says, "We're on the same side, Danny boy. Aren't we?"

We're not and he knows it, but he's daring me to take him on. He's a head taller and built like an athlete. Me, I'm a skinny bean in blurred glasses. A kid who's always managed to avoid a fight.

Until now.

12.

Two Red Eyes

When my little brothers start fighting, I can usually make them stop. Partly because I'm the oldest, but mostly because I'm bigger than they are. With me and Deke, it's just the opposite. That's why my knees are shaky as I step between him and Mia. My mouth is suddenly so dry it's hard to get the words out.

"Hey, Deke? Um, can I ask you a favor?"

He gives me this scornful look, like I must be out of my mind. "Seriously?"

"If we could talk for a minute?" I ask him.

He shakes his head, but allows me to turn him away from Mia, who's holding her ground. When we're a few yards away, he stops and folds his arms across his chest and says, "This better be good."

"Okay, first, we *are* on the same side. The side of finding our way home. Of, um, you know, surviving? And you can really help us do that. You're the biggest and the strongest, and out here in the wilderness, that could make all the difference."

"Blah blah blah. Do you have a point, Danny boy?"

"My point is, um, that we're counting on you. We're all hungry, but some of us are scared we'll run out of food. So if you keep leading us along the trail like you're doing, I'll give you some of my share of breakfast tomorrow morning."

Deke stares at me like I'm a bug on a windshield and he's the wiper. "Dude, that is so weak. I'm ashamed for you."

A few minutes later, he's back leading the hike, with Tony tagging just behind. Mia is so embarrassed for me that she doesn't bother to thank me for handling the situation. Imani must see it different, because she touches her forehead and nods in approval, as if to say, *Good thinking*.

What I did to distract Deke probably seems pitiful, at the very least. But it worked. He's fighting his way along the river, breaking new trail with his big feet and his long arms, and he and Tony seem to have given up on demanding another meal.

It won't last, I know that.

———————————

By midafternoon, the rain has eased, even if the sky stays so overcast that it feels like you could reach up and touch the clouds. Then, for a while, the pathway widens, making it much easier to trudge along. Mia looks like she's struggling

50

with the backpack, but the thought of asking if she wants a hand makes me cringe. Plus, it would crank Deke up. Better keep my mouth shut and hope we can get through the day.

How many miles have we hiked? Who knows? Probably not as many as it feels. All the times we've clambered down to drink from the river and then had to climb back up, that slows us down.

When daylight starts to dim, Imani suggests we look for shelter and make camp. We all seem to agree that's a good idea. Tony makes a joke of it. "Motel 6? Really? I think we need to aim higher."

Some of us chuckle, because it is sort of funny. Not Imani. "Like a cave or something," she says, dead serious. "Anything to stay dry."

With that in mind, we study the opposite side of the ravine, looking for the shadows that might mark a cave.

Tony prances around, making caveman noises. "Uga booga! Ug ug a jug!"

I'm not surprised that Mia spots the cave first. She has the sharpest eyes. The cave, if you can call it that, isn't in the face of the ravine. It's under a mass of roots from a toppled tree. Some big slabs of rock lifted up by the roots, and under that, what looks to be an area protected from the weather.

Mia gets the flashlight out of the backpack.

"Look out for bears," Tony jokes.

"Not funny."

Mia clicks on the flashlight and aims the beam into the opening.

Two glowing eyes stare back at us.

With a horrifying, catlike shriek, a mountain lion explodes from the darkness.

13.

Wild Yellow Eyes

The creature, all muscle and bone, lands in a crouch no more than ten feet from Mia. Ears back, tail twitching, jaws open to show big, glistening fangs. Hissing and growling, low in its throat, like a purr gone bad. All the signs of impending attack.

"Stand next to me!" I shout. "Don't break eye contact! Stare at it! Make yourself look tall! Raise your hands over your head! The bigger we look, the more chance it will run away."

We jam ourselves together, side by side, fists in the air. If Mia was alone, she'd probably already be dead. Fangs like that can penetrate a human skull. But confronted by five humans, the beast is nervous, unsure of itself.

The growl gets louder, higher. The tail twitches faster.

"Don't run. No matter how much you want to, don't. Running makes you look like a meal."

"So what do we do?" Tony sounds as scared as me.

"Back up slowly," I say, looking into the lion's yellow eyes. "Keep together."

We back up, putting a few yards between us and the lion. Its crouch tightens, as if preparing to pounce or charge.

"We yell together, at the top of our lungs," I say. "Not in fear, but in threat. 'Go, cat,' as loud as possible. All together now . . .

"GO, CAT! GO, CAT! GO, CAT!"

Those wild yellow eyes, drinking us in, wanting blood. Wanting to claw and tear and rip and bite.

We chant-scream, "GO, CAT! GO, CAT! GO, CAT! GO, CAT! GO, CAT!"

Now or never. I have a jackknife in my pocket, but don't dare lower my hands to take it out. Besides, a small knife isn't much of a weapon against a creature with fangs that big.

"GO, CAT! GO, CAT! GO, CAT! GO, CAT! GO, CAT!"

With a swish of its tail, the beast explodes from its crouch and runs away. So fast and furious that in the time it takes to exhale, the mountain lion has vanished.

My knees are so weak I nearly fall down.

Mia, sobbing in relief, gives me a hug that nearly breaks my ribs.

"Dude," Tony says, lowering his arms. "How did you know to do that?"

I shrug. "My brother Phil. He's two years younger, and when he heard about this trip, he was freaked out that I'd get eaten by mountain lions. Which almost happened, so thank you, Phil! Anyhow, to make him feel less scared for me, we looked it up together, what to do if confronted by a lion. Five things. Don't break eye contact. Make yourself look tall. Never run. Back up slowly. Shout as loud as possible."

Mia says, "I wanted to run."

"Worst thing you can do. It will trigger an attack for sure. Running down prey is what it does."

Deke gives me a punch to the arm, a little too hard to be friendly. "Pretty cool, Danny boy. Impressive. But you didn't have to worry. I could have killed it with my bare hands. Seriously. That skinny, mangy thing couldn't have weighed more than seventy pounds."

Imani, hands on her hips, confronts him. "Fool! You are a fool, Deke! A mean, stupid fool! You didn't save us, he did!"

Deke stares at her like he stared at the big cat. Then he laughs, whooping it up and clapping his hands. "Wow! She speaks!"

Imani shakes her head, disgusted.

He turns to me. "Hey, no hard feelings, Danny boy. I was just teasing."

It's obvious he doesn't mean the apology, that it's just more teasing, but I decide we've got more important things to do, like finding shelter, so I go, "No hard feelings. We, um, need to keep moving."

Deke gives me a scornful look. "Keep moving? We won

55

the cave. It's ours. We can build a fire, make a hot meal."

"Lions defend their lairs. It will come back."

He makes more of a fuss, but when the rest of us start moving, he does, too. And as we slog along, exhausted and hungry, searching for a place to get out of the rain, I'm thinking there's a creature even more dangerous than a mountain lion.

His name is Deacon Bailey, and if we're not careful, he's going to get us killed.

14.

No Reason to Starve

I'm hoping the mountain lion has had enough of us shouting humans and hightailed it in the opposite direction. But in case I'm wrong, we stick close together as we slowly hike away from the cave. Trudging along with the warm, misty rain dripping from the brim of my cap.

An hour or so later, night has fallen, and Mia suggests we call it a day. "Too dangerous to keep going in the dark. We'll just have to rig the tarp as best we can."

To my surprise, Deke decides to help. Mia holds the flashlight while we find branches to rig the lines. It's only a cheap blue tarp, one that has already started to leak, but it's better than nothing. Mia suggests we sit with our backs to each other, instead of lying on the damp ground, and try to get some sleep.

Tony finds the idea ridiculous. "Are you serious? What about making a fire? Eating a hot meal? I mean, after that freaking tiger, don't we deserve to celebrate?"

"It was a lion, Tony," says Mia.

"I don't care what it was. A thing with scary teeth that wanted to eat us."

"And we can't make a fire because we don't have any dry wood and it's too dark to find any. Without a fire, we can't boil water for the freeze-dried. Okay? We'll just have to wait for morning."

"Don't talk to me like I'm stupid! Deke, am I right? Help me out here."

"He's right," Deke says. "We deserve a fire and a meal."

"Sorry," Mia says softly, and a little sadly. "We wait until daylight."

What happens next is almost as scary as the lion. Deke leaps to his feet, his head thumping the tarp. He screams at Mia. Not words, just animal-like sounds of rage.

The darkness makes it scarier, to witness him out of control.

"I'm sick of this!" he rages. "Sick of you bossing us around! What do you know? You're just a girl! You think you're better than us! But you're not! You're a nothing!"

In my imagination, I picture myself decking him with one punch. But I'd never be able to do that in real life. He's too strong and angry. I'm too skinny and afraid.

"You act like we might never be rescued, and put yourself in charge of the food. You're the one who's stupid, Mia! Because there's a billionaire out there right now, searching for us. Byron James! He's paying for this trip, for the leadership program, you really think he isn't

58

going to spend whatever it takes to locate the survivors?"

"You tell her, Deke!" Tony chimes in, gleeful.

I decide I have to say something, even if it means he takes a swing at me. "Um, I sure hope you're right. I really do. But they don't have any idea we were on the Crazy River, or survived the flood from the broken dam. So like Mia said, maybe they're not looking here. Montana is a big state, right? Lots of wilderness to get lost in."

I can't see Deke's face, but no doubt he's sneering. "You don't know Byron James. I do. My parents work for the guy, remember? He's like a genius on a bunch of levels. The most important inventor since Edison, they say. He'll be checking every little detail, and he'll hire the best, most well-equipped search parties. By now they've figured out we weren't on that first river. They'll be looking at every white-water river in a hundred miles."

"I hope so."

"Guaranteed! They'll find us tomorrow, the next day at the latest. So there's no reason to starve. One last time, Mia. Give me the backpack. I don't care how dark it is, we'll scrounge up some wood and make a fire and eat until we're not hungry. Hand it over now."

Her answer is a whisper. "No."

"Fine! Be that way. I'm calling for a vote. Who leads the group, Mia or me?"

"What about Daniel?" Imani says. "Maybe he should be leader."

59

Deke laughs. The idea of me as leader is that funny. "Danny boy? Want to throw your hat in the ring?"

"No way."

"That's what I thought. Two choices, me or Little Miss Know-It-All. Ready? Mia, turn on the flashlight."

"We need to save the batteries."

"Turn it on! We can't have a show of hands in the dark."

She turns it on. And screams at what she sees.

15.

The War Begins

It's Tony, making a scary face, right in the beam of the flashlight.

"Gotcha!" he crows, pleased with himself.

We all laugh nervously, even Mia.

"That was awesome," Deke says, clapping Tony on the back. "I jumped a foot."

At first, I'm thinking Tony's prank has lightened the mood, that letting off steam is a good thing. At least Deke is no longer ranting. But it turns out he's still intent on taking over the backpack, or at least the food distribution, and he's determined that we should vote on it.

He props the flashlight on the ground so that we can see each other. Shadowed and distorted, but visible.

"This will be a leadership vote. You must choose, and we all agree to accept the result. Mia, do you agree?"

She looks around, trying to make eye contact with all of us. "Yes. I agree."

Deke says, "Raise your hand if you want Mia to be in charge."

Mia and Imani immediately raise their hands. That's two out of five. Three out of five means Mia wins.

I slowly raise my hand.

"What!" Deke is shocked at the result. "Are you serious? You're siding with the girls? Is something wrong with you? Are you mentally ill? That's it! That's the only explanation. You're a mental defective, like your wacky dad."

I'm stunned. Not by Deke's angry outburst—I expected that—but by the stuff about my dad. How does he know? I've never talked about it with anyone outside my family, except for the therapist my mother made me see. And I'm pretty sure a therapist is sworn to secrecy.

If Deke knows, then everybody knows. It feels like I'm sinking into the ground. Like I'm on a falling elevator. Falling, falling.

Part of me wants to attack Deke, and part of me wants to run away.

Weenie that I am, I don't do or say anything. But one thing is for sure, I'll never be the same again. This fall, I'm supposed to go to a brand-new regional middle school, full of kids I've yet to meet, and apparently all of them have already heard that my father has serious mental health issues.

Not going to happen. I'll tell Mom, and she'll have to make other arrangements. Send me to another school district, far enough away so they won't know my secret shame, that sometimes my father is so freaked out, so agitated, that he has to be confined.

It happened when I was nine years old, and I'll never ever forget it. My father in the state hospital for three weeks. It felt like forever.

Mia says to Deke, "That's so mean, what you said. What if it was you? How would you feel?"

He gives a cruel laugh. "Like throwing myself off a cliff."

Imani says, "Oh, stop, you rotten bully! You called for a vote and you lost. Get over it. We need to be a team. We need to help each other, not make fun of each other."

"Oh yeah? The person I need to help is me, okay? Because I'm sick of being hungry and I'm sick of some dumb little girl ordering me around. So that's what I'm going to do, help myself!"

Deke kicks the flashlight, and as Mia scrambles to retrieve it, he yanks the backpack away from her and shoves her to the ground.

"Mine," he says. "Believe it."

He slips the strap over his shoulder, steps out from under the tarp, and vanishes into the night.

"Wait for me!" Tony shouts. And a moment later, he's gone, too.

16.

Three Choices

It happened so fast we're stunned into silence. What can you say when the world turns upside down? We had a chance to survive by working together, by supporting each other, and Deke changed everything when he snatched the backpack and split us up.

Three against two. We outnumber them, but Deke and Tony together are stronger than we are, as he just proved.

Mia fumbles around and recovers the flashlight. "At least they didn't take the flashlight or the tarp."

"This is so messed up," I say. "What can we do?"

"If you want to change your vote, that's allowed."

I shake my head. Realizing that they can't see me, I say, "No way. I chose the right side. Deke's out of control, and that makes him dangerous. They'll get themselves killed."

Imani goes, "At least they'll die with full bellies. Assuming they can make a fire."

Mia says fiercely, "We have three choices. One: We do nothing. Stay where we are and hope to be rescued. Two: We follow the river like we planned, but without food or fire. Three: We wait until dawn, find the enemy, and take back what is ours."

"The enemy?" I ask.

"What else would you call them?"

I open my mouth, but can't think of what to say. She's right. If you shove a girl to the ground and steal from her, you are an enemy. If you leave her without food or fire, you are an enemy.

"So, what do you choose?" she wants to know.

Imani and I both say, "Three!"

We take back what is ours. If we can figure out how to do it.

The night seems to last a thousand years. Mia and Imani sound like they're sleeping. No way can I nod off. I'm too charged up, too worried. What if they come back to steal the tarp or the flashlight? What if the mountain lion is hunting for a midnight snack?

Weapon. I need a weapon. And I have one, sort of. My jackknife. Okay, it's a tool with a short blade for cutting and carving. But maybe it can be a weapon, too.

In the darkness, my imagination runs wild. I imagine confronting Deke and Tony with the jackknife, demanding they hand over the backpack. And then I imagine Deke yanking the knife out of my hands and stabbing me with my own weapon.

Ouch. Gross.

What I can't seem to imagine is *me* stabbing anyone. Not for food. Not for anything. That kind of violence makes me feel sick. Sorry, but you already know I'm a wuss. I'm bad at sports, I'd be even worse at war.

Forget the jackknife.

My stomach is growling, begging for food. I've never really been hungry before, not like this. Hunger is like a little brother tugging at my sleeve, begging for something to eat, keeping me awake. This is so lame, but I can't stop thinking about pancakes. The Mother's Day morning when me and my brothers wrecked the kitchen trying to make pancakes for Mom so she could have breakfast in bed. And how happy she was, despite the mess in the kitchen and the fact the pancakes tasted like rubber. How she gave us a group hug and said how lucky she was to have four wonderful sons, and that we were not to worry, because everything would be okay, even if it seemed scary sometimes.

That was the year Dad was in the hospital for almost a month, and we were all worried sick. To this day, I believe that group hug saved us, and kept the family together. Mom's magic hug made all the difference.

Eventually, I must have fallen asleep, because the next thing I know, the girls are nudging me awake.

"Hey, sleepyhead. Time to take back what's ours."

In the dim light of dawn, I can see that they're grinning at me, like they know something I don't. And they're both holding long wooden sticks, slender branches that look an awful lot like spears.

What's going on? What do they have in mind?

Mia stands at attention, shoulders back, chin up. "Maria Valentina Garcia, ready for battle."

"Is this a joke?"

"The opposite," Imani says, hefting her spear. "We assumed you'll be joining us."

"I've been thinking about that," I say miserably. "I don't think I can do it."

They look at each other, then look at me.

Imani says, "You stood up to a mountain lion, you can stand up to a bully and his clown. Let's go!"

Day Four

17.

Die! Die! Die!

Mia hands me one of the spears they made while I was asleep. It doesn't have a sharp end, so it's not like you could really hurt someone with it. But still, it looks like a weapon.

"Better than nothing," Imani says. "To defend ourselves."

"Right."

We march into the daylight brandishing our sticks. We're bad, wicked bad. Standing tall, unafraid. Well, pretending to be unafraid. Show fear to a bully, he'll use it against you.

"Which way?" Imani asks.

I shrug helplessly. It's not like I know anything about tracking.

"There," Mia says, pointing at a small strip of cloth stuck to the brambles.

We push carefully through the scratchy brambles and spot a trail of muddy footprints, heading back in the direction we came from yesterday. I put my finger to my lips.

We must be silent. They can't be far away. How far could they get in the dark of night without a flashlight?

We follow the footprints through the area of bushes, into a forest of slender aspen trees. The rain is a gentle mist, and almost feels good, washing away the grit and sweat of a long and mostly sleepless night. I snug the brim of my cap, convinced we're doing something important, something absolutely necessary. Defending ourselves. And I'm proud that my two companions have faith in me to do the right thing.

I hope I'm up to it. It's not like I have a lot of experience standing up to bullies. Like none. Up to now, if a bully picked on me, I did my best to avoid him.

Don't be surprised. I keep telling you I'm no hero. Once, when I was in fourth grade, an older kid grabbed my glasses and stomped them to bits. I never told the truth. Instead, I took the blame, claiming I broke my own glasses while fooling around on the jungle gym.

Glasses are expensive, and my dad wasn't working at the time. Mom sent me to bed early as punishment. All because I was afraid to tell on a kid who could stomp me like he stomped my glasses.

Mia points and whispers, "Over there."

Eyes of an eagle, that's Mia. Through the skinny aspens, she's spotted a place where a large stone slab juts out from a hillside. And there, under the slab, is the enemy. Deke and Tony sound asleep, stretched out like

72

they don't have a care in the world. Their campfire is still smoking. Pine branches from a tree that fell under the slab, out of the rain. As we get closer, we can see the water pan resting in the ashes, and a couple of empty freeze-dried food packages.

Mia is seething. The first thing these jerks did was eat twelve servings of food between them. Two full packages. No wonder they're sleeping like spoiled babies! But Mia will have to hold her temper. What's important is recovering the backpack, and whatever is left of the food.

Mia's plan of attack is that one of us sneaks up, as silently as possible, and takes the pack while they're sleeping. We discuss it quietly, and Imani is having none of it. "We need to scare them," she whispers fiercely. "Otherwise they'll attack us again. We have to end this right now, while we have the chance."

She has a better idea, and once she explains it, I know in my heart she's right.

Gripping our spears, we creep up on the sleeping boys. If only they knew what is about to happen. But they don't, and that's what gives us the advantage. On the silent count of three, we leap to our feet, shaking our "spears" like warriors and shrieking at the top of our lungs.

"DIE! DIE! DIE! DIE!"

Not that anyone is going to die, or even get hurt. It's all for show, to put the fear into them. They're on the ground, confused, waking up to a nightmare. We swarm all over them, screaming and stamping our feet and shaking our weapons.

They don't stand a chance.

Mia grabs the pack, Imani snatches the water pan, and we screech off into the forest.

The war isn't over, but we won the battle, and it sure feels good.

18.

Making a Fire

About a hundred yards from the enemy camp, we pause to catch our breath.

"What's next?" Imani wants to know.

"Daniel?" Mia asks. "Any ideas?"

"Grab the tarp and put some distance between us. We can't let them get ahead or they'll ambush us."

"I agree."

Imani runs back, grabs the tarp, and Mia tucks it into the backpack. "Ready? Let's go!"

We take off running.

Now that the attack is over, I'm scared to death. We threatened them with sticks that looked like spears. What will they do in revenge? Use real, sharpened spears? It wouldn't surprise me, and the fear of it helps me run. Not flat-out running, I can't keep that up for long. More like jogging. We're following the path of least resistance, avoiding thick woodlands and underbrush that might slow us down, but trying not to stray too far from the river.

Lose the river and we'll truly be lost.

Jogging in the misty rain on an empty stomach—not my idea of a fun adventure. I pretend we'll find a restaurant along the way. An old-style twenty-four-hour breakfast diner like we have in New Hampshire. I'll order pancakes and eggs and sausage and toast and home fries and a big glass of cold milk.

I never had a goal in life, not really, but I do now. If we survive this, I never want to be hungry again.

I don't know how long we keep going, but it feels like hours. Eventually, Imani begs us to stop. She has a pain under her ribs and can't go on, not without resting for a while.

"Fine," Mia says. "Daniel, can you help me rig the tarp? We need to eat something."

Like before, finding dry kindling is a problem. By the time I gather enough for a fire, Mia has emptied out the backpack. Turns out Deke and Tony did even more damage than we expected. In addition to gorging on the freeze-dried meals, they used all the fire-starter cubes.

"Who would do that?" Mia says, more in wonder than in anger.

"Someone who believes they'll be rescued today. No need to plan for tomorrow if helicopters are on the way."

Mia snorts. "Have you heard any helicopters?"

"Just saying."

"So how do we start a fire?" I ask.

She hands me the tin box containing the fire-starter

76

kit. The easy-to-light cubes may be gone, but we still have waterproof matches and the flint stick for striking sparks. I'm so hungry my hands are shaking, so it takes three matches to coax a flame in a pile of slightly damp leaves.

Please don't go out. Please, please, please.

The leaves are barely burning when I add twigs and carefully blow on the smoky pile that's going to save our lives.

Come on, flames. Come on, fire.

The girls are watching, not saying anything. Hope in their eyes. They trust me, which is amazing. Nobody outside of my family has ever needed to trust me. It makes me anxious but proud.

When our little fire is strong and true, I place a pan of rainwater above the flames and wait for it to boil. The smoke from the fire, trapped under the tarp, makes my eyes water, but it's a small price to pay for a life-giving fire.

Imani clears her throat. "I was thinking, how did Deke find that shelter last night? In the dark, without a flashlight?"

Mia cocks her head, considering it. Then she nods to herself. "He knew where he was going. He already knew it was there!"

I agree. "That must be it. He spotted a good shelter when we were hiking but didn't tell us because he was saving it for himself. In case he lost the vote. He was planning to steal the backpack all along."

The water comes to a boil, and we pour it into the food pouch. Ten minutes until it's ready. My stomach is begging, *Feed me feed me feed me.*

"It means he plans ahead," Imani says, very serious.

Mia nods. "It means he's even more dangerous than we thought."

At last, we eat, before the enemy can spoil our appetites.

19.

Something Shining

We give up on jogging—the stitch in Imani's side is still bothering her—and concentrate on fast walking. Putting miles between us and the enemy. Or so we hope. There's no predicting what Deke might do. Except that one way or another he'll want to get the food back under his control.

Food. Mushy-tasting freeze-dried food. Hard to believe that's what this war is all about. It may seem stupid—it *is* stupid—but try not eating for a few days and maybe you'll understand. Hunger takes over your brain. It's all you can think about when you're awake, and all you dream about when you're asleep.

Food, food, food.

"We have seven packages left," Mia reminds us when we take a short break. "Six if we leave one behind for the enemy."

"What? You'd do that?"

She shrugs. "I'd think about it. Deke is a bully and a thief, but that doesn't mean he should starve. And Tony,

79

he's just . . . wrong. Trying to be friends with the wrong person."

"They ate twelve meals between them. They're hardly starving."

"Not today and maybe not tomorrow. But if we haven't been rescued by the third day, we'll take a vote on sharing."

"A vote? The last one didn't go so good."

That makes Imani roll her eyes. "Didn't go so good" doesn't come close to describing what happened.

"Better keep moving," I suggest. "You-know-who may be catching up."

We find ourselves climbing along the edge of a higher ravine, looking down at the river below. Not as much flood debris as we saw before. What there is has been washed up at the sharp curves of the river. Piles of uprooted trees, heaps of gravel. Boulders that must have rolled for miles when the dam broke.

"Did you see that?" Mia says, pointing toward the river with her spear.

"What?" I ask, fearful that she's spotted the enemy about to attack.

"Something shining. Under those logs."

I squint at where she's pointing. Yes, there's something down there. Not a log or a boulder. Something that shines.

Metal.

Climbing down from the top of the ravine takes a while. Falling is not an option, so we're forced to go slow. Using our spears as walking sticks. Helping each other along the trail, heading for the curve of the river.

The piles of debris loom bigger and bigger, the closer we get.

"It's probably nothing," I say, not wanting to get our hopes up.

Mia grunts. She hasn't said much since pointing out the shiny thing, but she's determined to find it, as if she thinks it might be useful, whatever it is. Imani is even more solemn than usual. Like she's worried that it will be a bad thing or a sad thing.

It turns out to be a sad thing.

"There, under that pile!"

I climb over the splintered trees, lowering myself almost to water level. The river is still a river, even though it's clogged with broken things. And what Mia spotted is as broken as it can get. So broken it takes me a while to figure out what I'm looking at.

Sky Hanson's transport van, crushed like a soda can in a cement mixer.

20.

A Sky Full of Stones

It's hard to believe that we were once passengers in this crushed and ruined hunk of metal.

"Poor Sky," Imani says. "He was a good guy. What they did was so brave."

The van had once been white, but most of the paint has been scraped away, leaving bare steel. All the windows are missing, there's a long gash in the roof, and what's left of the vehicle is swamped in about three feet of water. The tires are gone, ripped from the hubs. The seats have been mushed together.

"Anything inside? I remember there was gear in the back. Maybe stuff we didn't need on the river trip, but might come in handy now." Mia sounds almost wistful.

Hanging on to a branch, I reach down as far as I can. Plunging my free hand into the water. Being careful because of all the jagged metal edges. My fingers find a plastic handle, and I lift out the blue cooler. The one that had all the snacks.

It's very heavy. Way too heavy.

Imani and Mia help me lift it free. We crack the lid. No surprise, the snacks are gone and the cooler is full of water and sand.

"Keep looking. There must be more."

I manage to get down into the wrecked vehicle, kneeling on what remains of the seats. Fishing around the muddy water, I recover the following treasures:

A battered aluminum coffeepot. A coil of black rope. A tin box that's the twin of our fire-starter box. A University of Montana baseball cap. A set of Allen wrenches. A utility knife.

"It's got to be there," Mia says, sounding desperate.

"What's got to be there?"

"There was a cardboard box that I'm pretty sure contained packets of freeze-dried. I remember because I had to move it to make room and Sky said put it in the back."

That explains her keen interest. Food. But if the box was in the back when we left the van, it's long gone, torn loose by the flood. I tell her as much but she doesn't believe me, and gets down into the water to check for herself.

She splashes around in frustration, coming up empty. I exchange a glance with Imani, who shrugs as if to say, *There's no stopping Mia when she gets an idea in her head.*

While she's searching, I check out the fire-starter box. There's water inside, but the matches are in sealed, waterproof containers. Good. And the waxy fire-starter cubes are ready to ignite. Excellent. For this alone it was worth the long climb down. Add in the rope and the utility knife, it's a major find.

Imani seems to be most interested in the aluminum coffeepot. She checks it out, and despite being battered and bent, it still holds water. "For boiling," she says.

"We already have one."

"We can leave it for the enemy, as a peace offering." Her expression is solemn, serious. She's given it some thought.

Mia, when she finally accepts that there are no food packets in the wrecked van, agrees. "We leave them the pot, matches, one packet of freeze-dried. Less reason for them to attack, if they have food and a way to cook it."

I'm not so sure. My guess is, it doesn't matter what we give him, Deke wants it all.

Working our way around the splintered trees, we find our way back to the base of the ravine. It's going to be harder going up than coming down, but maybe the rope we recovered will be useful. I'm thinking we should yoke ourselves together for the climb, just to be on the safe side, when a rock hits the ground at my feet.

Barely missed my head. I look up to see where it came from, and suddenly the sky is full of stones.

"Surrender!" Deke shouts from the top of the ravine. "Surrender or die!"

21.

Run or Die

I gotta say, an enemy raining stones down on your head is even scarier than confronting a mountain lion. We flee in panic, screaming for them to stop, and take refuge behind a cluster of shattered trees.

It's a miracle none of us got injured. Unless they're throwing not to kill, but to scare. To force our surrender. Once we're a safe distance away, we scan the top of the ravine and spot Deke and Tony, stones in their fists and grins upon their faces.

"Give up, losers!" Deke struts along the edge, brandishing his rocks. "Next time we won't miss! And don't even think about shaking those stupid spears because rocks break sticks!"

He slams the stones together, making his point. He looks jubilant up there, on top of the world.

Mia's voice is hushed. "Imani? Daniel? Any ideas?"

"Not really. If we run away, they'll keep following us. And maybe next time we get hurt. Or worse."

Imani says, "We give them something, like we talked

about. And then we get as far away from them as we can."

From the top of the ravine, Deke shouts, "You better be talking about surrender, because that's the only way this ends!"

Tony's job seems to be gathering rocks. He has quite a pile ready to go.

Mia unzips the backpack and prepares an offering, as Imani suggested. I feel like I should say something, make a plea for sanity, but don't want to make things worse. But I can't stop myself.

"Deke! Deke, this is crazy! We're stronger together than apart!"

He shakes his head. "You had your chance and you blew it! You voted to stay with those losers!"

Tony lopes along the edge, chanting, "*Lose*-ers! *Lose*-ers! Stupid girly *lose*-ers!"

Mia says, "I've got this, Daniel."

She moves out from behind the cluster of broken trees, holds up the coffeepot, and lifts the lid. "For you! Two packages of freeze-dried! See? Twelve portions! A jar of matches! A pot to boil water! Come and get it!"

Deke screams, "I WANT IT ALL!"

Mia sets the pot down on the very edge of the river, within inches of moving water. "This won't stay here for long! The river will steal it! Hurry if you want to eat today!"

Up top, Deke and Tony are conferring. Deke points

down and Tony nods. Then they back away from the edge, out of our sight.

"Hurry!" Mia urges us.

Imani and I catch up as she jogs along the riverbank. We have our spears, but we also have no doubt they'll be useless if the enemy makes it down from the top of the ravine before we're gone. Deke has that part right. His stones will crush our spears, and our skulls, if his aim is true.

As soon as we get to a clear part of the riverbank, with no debris blocking our path, we start to run. None of us need to say a word. We know what the stakes are.

Life or death. Run or die.

22.

The Queen of Not Giving Up

We run for miles. We run until we drop to our knees, until Imani cries from the pain under her ribs.

Mia scoops water from the river and lets the sand settle to the bottom of the pan. "We have to drink plenty of water. Slurping rainwater is fine, but we need to keep hydrated."

"Do you think they took the bait?" I ask.

"It's not bait, Daniel. That was sharing. But I hope so."

Imani has recovered her breath enough to say, scornfully, "Are you serious? They'll be stuffing their bellies by now. I bet they ate all twelve portions, like they did last time."

Mia agrees. "Deke is cruel and greedy. But he understands we offered him a lifeline."

"That doesn't mean he'll give up," Imani insists. "We're following the same river, heading for the same place. He'll find us."

Mia nods. "You're right. We need to keep a watch. Don't let them sneak up on us again."

We agree to be vigilant, and to keep moving. We bump

our spears, give a quiet cheer, and continue on, fast as we can walk.

The Crazy River bends so sharply that sometimes it almost reverses direction. We decide to climb up for a better view and find ourselves hiking along the very edge of the ravine, looking down at curls of white in the water below. A few miles back, the river was clotted with broken trees and boulders, but not here. Too far from where the dam broke? That's Imani's theory.

"Maybe the force of the flood got slowed down by all the twists and turns? Or it just used itself up. The dam may be gone, but the flow of water is still amazing. All the rain, it powers the river."

Mia agrees. "If we had a raft, we could use it for sure."

I study the curve of the river. From above, you can see how it erodes the ravine walls, reshaping itself. Almost like the river is alive. I guess in a way, it is.

"What if we made a raft?" Imani suggests. "Use the rope we found to tie some logs together."

The idea hits me like a surge of electricity. Yes!

"You're a genius!" I give her a quick hug. She winces, clutching her side. "Sorry! Sorry, sorry!"

She shakes off the apology. Mia is already checking the backpack for the black rope retrieved from the remains of Sky's van. "You think this is strong enough? Will it hold?"

There's only one way to find out.

It takes us the rest of the day to climb down to river level and find a few logs that are the right size. Big enough to float three kids, but small enough so we can drag them into place. If we had a saw or a hatchet, it would be a lot easier, but we don't.

"We work with what we have. What's in the pack and what's up here," Mia says, tapping her forehead. "Have you ever built a log raft, Daniel?"

"No," I admit.

She grins, eyes sparking with energy. "Me neither! There's always a first time, right?"

The hardest part is figuring out how to use the rope. The logs need to be lashed together, tight as can be, and that's a lot easier said than done. The knots keep slipping and the rope loosens, no matter how many times we wrap it around each log. Our raft keeps falling apart, even before it gets launched into the surging river.

Makes me wish I was a Scout. They learn about knots, I think.

Mia finally comes up with the idea of winding it tight, which is brilliant. We use a short stick, push it into the loose rope between logs, and then wind the stick until the rope tightens.

Mia sasses Imani, "Now who's the genius? It is I, Maria Valentina Garcia, queen of not giving up!"

We're sweaty and exhausted—not to mention hungry—and agree the launch should wait until morning. That way we'll have the whole day to ride the current downriver, and keep clear of Deke and Tony, who are no doubt trying to catch up to us.

"By this time tomorrow, we'll be at our destination," Imani says confidently. "Heck, we could be in a helicopter, heading home. Or a private jet—wouldn't that be cool?"

We all agree it would be cool, whatever the form of transportation. It's fun imagining our rescue.

What we didn't know is how wrong we were.

23.

The Viz

We've gotten good at finding dry kindling. This time we build a fire bigger than we need to boil water. Big enough to make us feel warm and safe, and a little sleepy after we fill our bellies with freeze-dried rice and chicken.

Raft building has left us so exhausted that at first no one has much to say. But when it's dark enough that we can barely see each other in the flames of the fading fire, Mia clears her throat. "I've been thinking."

"Uh-oh," I joke. "Danger zone."

She ignores me. "We worked together so great today, but really we barely know each other. We need to share, because that's what friends do. Since this is my idea, I'll go first." She takes a deep breath. "I was born with a hole in my heart. I was supposed to die, but this surgeon, Dr. Maria DeFranco, she decided to try an operation that had never been done before, not on newborns like me, and it worked. Because of her, I'm alive."

"And your heart is okay now?" Imani sounds concerned.

"Totally normal."

92

I say, "That's why your name is Maria?"

"Yes, that's why my name is Maria. Okay, Daniel, your turn. Tell us something about you we don't already know."

Normally I'd never share personal stuff about my family, but this isn't a normal type situation. Maybe that's why I blurt out, "My dad has bipolar disorder."

Silence. I'm starting to think I've made a terrible mistake, when Imani says, very softly, "I'm not sure what that is," and Mia adds, "Me neither."

"It's a mental illness. Sometimes if his medicine isn't working, or he forgot to take it, he gets super excited and talks a mile a minute about stuff that doesn't make sense. Then after a few days it all crashes down and he's so depressed he can't get out of bed or take care of us."

"That's terrible."

"Yeah. My mom has to work the late shift as a registered nurse so she can see us off to school and be there when we get back."

"She sounds amazing," Imani says.

"She is. She's the best mom in the world, and my dad tries really hard, but he can't help it, you know? It's not his fault."

"It's okay, Daniel. Really. Thanks for telling us."

We all stare at the fire for a while, thinking about stuff, until Imani finally takes her turn. "My secret is, I know why the search parties haven't found us."

"How could you know that?"

"Because I know about the viz," she says confidently.

"What's the viz?"

"Viz is short for visibility, which is really important for flying helicopters. My dad was a pilot in the marines, and he talked about how dangerous it was flying in low viz, especially in mountain country. Did you notice the clouds have been so low we can't see the mountaintops? Sometimes we can't see the mountains at all. I'm pretty sure search and rescue would be grounded in weather like this."

"The viz. Wow. Who knew?" Mia sounds amazed.

It *is* amazing, that Imani would know about helicopters, but even more amazing is the clever way she avoided sharing anything really personal. Maybe next time. It doesn't matter if she doesn't talk about her family, because I know I can trust her with my life. Mia, too.

I fall asleep with my head on my knees and dream that I'm already on the river. Not on a raft, but floating in a swim tube. My whole family is with me. My little brothers, my mom and dad. We're floating together, going slowly around and around in our swim tubes. We're so happy, and our laughter sounds like the river.

Day Five

24.

Hang On

The dawn is murky and dim. The sun can barely make it through the thick rain clouds. We're so pumped to try out the raft that we decide to postpone breakfast until later in the day. Staying ahead of the enemy is more important than filling our bellies.

The raft is way too heavy to lift, so we put smaller logs under it as rollers. That was Imani's suggestion. I'm getting the idea she's good at math and science and geometry. Stuff like that. Not exactly my strong area. I'm more about daydreaming and drawing.

We shove the raft, pushing with all our might, and Imani's plan works. The raft rolls slowly over the smaller logs and slips into the shallow water at the edge of the river. Mia ties the raft to the trunk of a tree, to keep it from drifting off before we're ready to go.

"We don't have life jackets, so it's super important nobody lets go of the ropes," Mia says, tightening the straps on her backpack. "Does everybody know how to swim?"

"I can do the crawl," Imani says.

"Daniel?"

"Dog paddle. But I can keep my head above water."

She rolls her eyes. "Just stay on the raft, please."

Mia unties the rope. We give the raft a shove and climb on, gripping the ropes. We don't have a paddle, so the raft is on its own, free to move with the current. At first, we remain close to shore, in knee-deep water, barely moving. Slowly we drift away from the riverbank, and the speed increases.

"This is so great!" Mia shouts. "Thank you, Imani! Thank you, Daniel!"

The three of us are seated with our knees up, clinging to the black ropes that tie the logs together. Sort of like riding a horse—not that I've ever ridden a horse. We're seeing the world go by at just above water level. The view from the top of the ravine was so different, it's like from another world.

As the raft drifts into the middle of the river, we start going even faster. It's working! We're making better progress than we could possibly do on foot. It seems entirely possible that by the end of the day we'll get where we need to go. The pickup location for rafting expeditions, which means a road and rescue.

I'm grinning so hard it almost hurts. I'm thinking how great it will be to get back home, see my little brothers and my mom and dad. The stories I'll have to tell. The flood, the lion, the crazy fight with the bully who almost wrecked everything.

And the raft. Especially the raft. How we built it all by ourselves, working together from start to finish. If only my family could see me now, riding the Crazy River! I wonder what my dad would think. Would it make him proud? Would it help him get better?

One thing for sure, once I'm back home, I'm going to finish my special project. Months ago, I got this idea for a graphic novel called *What's Wrong with My Dad*. At first, I was really excited, and drew a bunch of panels about why Dad had to go back to the hospital last year, where they put him on a new medicine to help with his bipolar disorder. But my drawing sucked, so I stopped working on it.

"Daniel! Wake up!"

Mia is looking at me with concern.

"I wasn't asleep, are you kidding?"

"You were a million miles away. We need to know if you can hear it, too."

"Hear what?"

"Just listen!"

I realize I've been hearing it for a while. A distant roaring that echoes off the ravine walls. I know that sound, we heard a lot of it that first day on the river.

White-water rapids, dead ahead.

"Hang on!" I scream. "Stay on the raft!"

25.

Fear-of-Dying Scared

Rivers get crazy when they flow downhill. Everything speeds up, and the boil of waves gives off a mist that charges the air with an electric smell. Our log raft begins to buck and bob as if alive. We're thrown from side to side, desperate to keep balance.

What had been fun in the inflatable raft, with a guide in charge, is out-of-control terrifying when you have no way to steer.

"STAY IN THE MIDDLE!" Mia screams.

I think she means stay as close to the center of the raft as possible. We're scraping past rocks that protrude from the thrashing water. Get your foot in the way and you might lose it.

Imani has this fierce look, like she's trying to calm the water with her eyes. Her dreads are soaked. We're all drenched, which makes it more difficult to hang on to the rope with slippery hands.

The raft pivots around as we enter a whirlpool. We're flying backward through the roaring waves, which means we can't see what's coming.

I've never been so scared in my life. Not fun scared. Fear-of-dying scared.

Mia yells something, but her words are swallowed by the roar of the rapids. I'm getting splashed in the face, so my glasses are blurry. Good thing they have an elastic strap or they'd be torn from my face.

Blind and careening backward, it's all I can do to hang on.

Suddenly we enter calmer water and the raft starts to spin the other way. I assume the worst is over. That's good because my arms are shaking from the effort of holding tight to the rope. But the river is playing tricks. The white water isn't done with us, not yet.

Boom, we're back in it! The logs leap and shift under us as we crash from rock to rock. I can't see a thing. I try to wipe my glasses without letting go of the rope, but it's impossible.

It's all I can do not to cry out for my mom. Not that anybody could hear me if I did. Is this how my dad feels when he's out of control? Terrified and excited at the same time?

It's like the river wants to wreck us. Like it's throwing a tantrum as it tries to tear the raft apart.

Please stop. Make it stop. Please please please!

I thought that building a raft was a great idea. What a moron. I never thought it through, what white-water rapids

101

could do to a runaway raft. No paddles, no ability to steer, no life jackets. What were we thinking?

A wave smashes into my open mouth, choking me. I cough so hard I almost fall off. Imani snags my shirt and yanks me back from the edge. Thank you thank you. Not that I can tell her because I'm still coughing.

"LOOK OUT!" Mia screams.

My glasses clear just enough to see what she means. We're speeding into a sharp curve where the waves break against the ravine wall. Nothing we can do to control the raft. We're completely at the mercy of waves and a raging current, heading right for the wall.

If we hit it, we'll be killed.

At the last possible second, a wave pushes us sideways. The logs scrape the ravine wall, and then we're back in the middle.

The worst must be over *now*, right?

Wrong. Because an eddy snatches the raft, pulling us toward the opposite shore. The river suddenly takes a steep drop. We plunge into the foaming rapids, and for a moment, the raft is underwater, sinking out from under us. Then it rises, tipping us backward, and crashes forward again.

Something is wrong. The ropes that hold the raft together are loosening. And dead ahead, a huge rock. We're aiming right at it, carried on the crest of a wave.

We slam into the rock. Imani and Mia shoot over the top and land on the sandy shore. I'm thrown sideways, my hands tangled in the rope. I want to get off, try to swim to the shore, but I can't.

I'm tied to the dying raft as the waves tear it apart. The separated logs twirl into the raging current, and I'm dragged underwater by the tangle of ropes.

Can't breathe. Can't see.

If I can't get loose, I'll drown.

26.

Hands from Heaven

Your life is supposed to flash before you if you're about to die. What flashes before me is my family. My little brothers, Phil, Jon, and Mark. In my mind, they're laughing, which is something they do a lot. Mom looks worried, because that's typical for her. And Dad is apologizing, as usual. *Sorry, Son, I'll get better, I promise.*

I miss them so much!

Then do something to stay alive. Try harder.

I'm below the surface of a raging river, tangled in a rope. The broken raft is dragging me under. Holding my breath feels like a big clamp tightening on my chest.

In about five seconds, I'll drown. The surge of terror gives me enough strength to pull my arm free of the rope. I bob to the surface just long enough to take a breath, then one of the tumbling logs bumps me back under.

Got to get away from the logs!

I'm kicking with all my might, struggling to keep my head above the waves. But like I said, I'm not much of a swimmer. I hate it when water goes up my nose, that was my excuse for avoiding swimming lessons.

It doesn't help that I can't see. Which way to the shore? No idea. No idea about much of anything, other than staying alive.

The dog paddle is getting me nowhere. My body decides to quit trying to escape from the raging current. Keeping my head up requires all of my strength. I'm fighting the river that wants to pull me under. The crazy, crazy river.

The river that killed the grown-ups has decided to kill the kids. Which doesn't make any sense—a river can't think—but my brain is so confused and dizzy that it's looking for reasons not to die.

Don't give up. Keep bobbing, grabbing a breath when you can.

Daniel Redmayne, don't let go! Remember who you are. Who cares about you. Stay alive. Use your panic to keep breathing. Don't inhale the water, no matter how much you are tempted.

Keep kicking. Keep rising. Grab air when you can.

I'm trying, but part of me says to give up. It's too exhausting, my strength is fading. The river will put me to sleep. The crazy, crazy river promises it won't hurt.

Crazy, crazy. Sorry, Dad. I understand now that you've been in your own crazy river, struggling to stay alive. Thank you for trying so hard. Sorry, but I'm going to give up and go to sleep.

Take a nap. The water will be my pillow. The river will rock me to sleep. It sings to me, a beautiful chorus of watery voices.

Dan-yul, *Dan*-yul, let it go, go to sleep, *Dan*-yul, *Dan*-yul.

Shhh, shhh, sleep is waiting, nothing to fear.

Dan-yul, *Dan*-yul.

That's it. It's over. I'm fading away. The light glowing through the water is so soft and beautiful.

I'm not afraid. I'm letting go.

And then two hands from heaven reach through the glowing water, and they lift me out of the river and bring me back to life.

It hurts!

27.

Friends for Life

The air is sweet, but I swallowed so much water I can barely inhale. Mia and Imani encourage me to get on my hands and knees so I can cough up the water. That's the part that hurts. Eventually there's nothing left to cough up and I start breathing like a normal person.

"Wow" is all I can manage to say.

Mia giggles. "Wow, he says. And wow it is! Imani did it, Daniel. She figured out how to save you."

"Thank you."

"It was amazing. We're racing along the shore, trying to keep up with you, but the river kept taking you away. Imani goes, 'Not on my watch!' and then she scrambles up the ravine, runs across to the next bend, and waits for you to drift by."

Imani shrugs, as if it's no big deal. "The shortest distance between two points is a straight line. I just cut through the curve and there you were."

"However you figured it out, you saved my life for sure."

"Like you saved ours. More than once."

Mia leaps to her feet. "Come on, I've got an idea, and it's really, really important!"

I get to my feet, still a bit woozy and weak in my knees.

"Join hands," Mia commands.

We link our hands. I'm feeling kind of shy, and Imani is acting cautious, but Mia's enthusiasm is contagious.

"This is a friendship circle. A sacred friendship circle that can never be broken. We have survived by relying on each other, by trusting each other, by saving each other. What we have shared makes us friends for life. Not for a summer, or for a school year. For life!"

She raises our hands in the air, and we join in her exclamation. "For life!"

I'm still soaking wet, so I'm pretty sure no one notices the tears in my eyes. I've never had friends like these two.

Not even close.

———————

The amazing thing is, Mia managed to keep hold of the backpack. When they got ejected from the raft and landed on the shore, it was firmly strapped around her shoulders. A lot of the stuff inside got pretty damp, but we'd been expecting that. Damp is what we are, all the time. I'm almost afraid to take off my shoes and look at my feet, because it feels like mushrooms are growing between my toes. Or maybe webs, like a duck.

Anyhow, we make another fire to help dry our clothes

108

and boil water for the freeze-dried. Mia says after our ordeal we need calories. Once I get a whiff of cooked rice, my belly starts begging to be fed. I'd almost forgotten how hungry I was before the raft dragged me underwater. That explains the weakness in my knees and the woozy feeling almost as much as nearly drowning.

We're half-starved. To be truthful, the food in the pouch tastes gunky, but nobody cares. We wolf it down, breathing through our noses and grunting with satisfaction.

When I've had my fill, I lie back and groan. "That was the best meal I've ever had. Better than pancakes and sausage."

"Eeew!" Imani makes a face. "Sausage is disgusting. Do you know what's in sausage?"

"No, and please don't tell me. Starving people eat all kinds of revolting things. Beetles, ants, worms. Anything to stay alive. The Donner party ate each other, that's how hungry they were."

"No way. You're making that up."

"True story. A wagon train of settlers heading west. They got stuck in the mountains, snowed in for the winter with not enough food. So they improvised."

Both girls go, "Eeew!"

"Don't worry, I could never be a cannibal. I'd rather die than eat liver of any kind."

That gets them laughing.

What a day this has been! Almost dying but somehow surviving, and making friends for life. And making them laugh, that's the icing on the cake.

What none of us know is that the fun is about to end, in the worst way possible.

28.

One for All and All for One

The meal makes us stronger, no doubt about it. Humans need fuel. I mean, duh, right? But for some reason I never understood what it meant to be starving. Really starving, not just hungry because you missed snack time.

The meal also makes one of us more talkative.

"You know what?" Imani says as we resume our march beside the river. "We're a team, right? And teams have a name. I vote we call ourselves the Dream Team."

"Where does that come from?" Mia asks.

She grins, her eyes lighting up. "My dad is a huge basketball fan, and the original Dream Team is his favorite of all time. The team that won the 1992 Olympics. He watches the final game every year on his birthday, and every year, he stands up and cheers when they win."

"I like it," Mia says. "Daniel?"

"Are you kidding? I've never been on any team, never mind a dream team. It's an honor."

I'm not really a loner type, but I don't have many friends, and until now, none of them were girls. Plus, I don't have a sister, so basically I'm clueless about girls. But it turns out having two wicked-smart, courageous girls for friends is totally great.

It's like we've been friends forever, even before we knew each other. Doesn't make sense, but that's how it feels. For instance, it doesn't seem weird at all that Mia likes to turn things into funny, cheerful songs, especially when we're hiking. That's who she is.

"One for all and all for one," she sings. "Keep on walking, have some fun. Please stop raining, come on, sun. One for all and all for one."

Imani joins in, and when I don't, she nudges me.

"Um, sorry, but I sound like a frog."

"Come on, Froggy. Sing!"

I do, and they think it's hilarious, but that's fine because I love to make them laugh. Because I know in my heart they're not laughing at me, we're laughing together.

One for all and all for one. What a beautiful idea.

We make good progress, tramping the shoreline, until the shoreline ends. As it comes to a curve, the river widens all the way to the ravine wall. We have to go back up top. Imani finds us a path, and we carefully work our way along it, using a rope for safety. The path is steep, and the ravine is high in this part of the river. At least fifty feet. Makes me wish I had hiking boots instead of soggy running shoes. But I don't, so I have to make do. One step at a time, don't slip. Slip and you're dead, or at least broken.

Reminds me that we're on the edge. The edge of the ravine wall and the edge of life. Break an ankle and it's all over. I decide if something like that happens to me, if I get injured, I'll tell the girls to go on without me. Send back a rescue crew when you get there. I'll be fine. I won't be, but that's what I'll tell them.

The top, when we get there, is heavily wooded. A forest of tall pine trees. The floor of the forest is thick with fresh-smelling pine needles.

"Let's take a breather," I suggest.

Mia is dropping the backpack to the ground, when a screaming attack explodes from behind the trees.

"DIE! DIE! DIE! DIE!"

The enemy is upon us.

29.

All the Way Down

Deke charges like a linebacker attacking a dummy. And I'm the dummy, slammed to the ground so hard it knocks the wind out of me. Before I can react, he has me pinned. I'm not strong enough to break free and can only watch as Tony pushes Mia down and snatches up the backpack.

"I got it! I got it!" he shouts gleefully.

From out of nowhere, Imani swarms Deke, jumping on his back. Her eyes are fierce.

"Let him go, you big bully! Let him go!"

Deke shakes her off and leers at me. "I never knew she cared! Is she your little girlfriend, Daniel? K-i-s-s-i-n-g?"

Imani says, "You are such a jerk! We left food for you! Doesn't that count for anything?"

Deke laughs, very pleased with himself. "That was fine while it lasted, but now we're hungry again. You had your chance. It's my turn, and by the law of the jungle, I take what I want."

"Law of the jungle?" She's scornful.

"It means survival of the fittest. The strongest survive. And that's me."

Mia shouts, "Tony, don't! You're too close! Get back!"

She's worried because Tony is prancing along the edge of the cliff, dangerously close. He swings the backpack back and forth, back and forth. "Deke! Deke! Look at me!"

He twirls around, like the pack is a hammer he's about to toss. Then, so quick I almost don't see it happen, his feet slip on the pine needles. As he loses his balance, he drops the pack, and tries to regain his footing, but it's too late.

Tony falls over the edge. He screams all the way down.

30.

Say Hello to Deacon Bailey

After the scream, there's nothing but silence, terrible silence. We're shocked into silence, too, because something too awful to think about has happened. That scream, it changes the world. It changes everything.

I crawl to the edge and look over. Tony lies at the bottom of the ravine, twisted and broken between two boulders. He's not moving. A wavy sick feeling passes from my head to my belly. It's all I can do not to throw up.

"I better check," I announce, my voice shaking. "Maybe he's still alive."

Mia says, "Don't, Daniel. What if you fall, too?"

"I won't."

I'm as careful as possible, finding my way down the cliff. From handhold to foothold. Concentrate on what you're doing, don't think too far ahead. Taking my time because I dread what I'll find when I get there. I've never seen a dead body. The thought terrifies me. But somebody has to do it. Tony Meeks was acting stupid and showing off, but he doesn't deserve to be abandoned. And maybe, just maybe, he's still alive.

At the bottom, I take a deep, shuddering breath and steel myself to the task. The boulders where he fell are not far away. The first thing I see are his feet, sticking out from behind the rock. Utterly and completely still.

I'm not an expert, but I don't really think anyone could survive a fifty-foot fall onto rocks. It turns out I'm right, but it's still hard to believe. Minutes ago he was dancing on the edge of the cliff, alive and full of mischief. Now he's gone, truly gone. The thing that surprises me, that shocks me almost as much as the accident, is that Tony isn't there. The body he left behind is badly damaged, but empty of poor Tony. I make myself find his wrist and feel for a pulse, just to be sure.

Nothing. The body is limp and lifeless. He's gone.

Imani shouts from the cliff top. "Daniel! Anything?"

I shake my head, take a deep breath. "I'm going to pile some rocks around, to protect him from animals! Are you and Mia okay?"

"Not really! But we're hanging in!"

"What about Deke?"

"He's not going anywhere!"

I'm not sure what that means, but first things first. I gather smooth rocks and stones from along the riverbank and carry them to Tony's temporary grave. Temporary, because I'm sure his family will want him closer. It takes a

117

long time to gather enough stones, but I keep at it, like a robot following my own commands.

Don't stop until it's done. He made a horrible mistake trying to impress Deke, but he deserves to be treated like a human, and humans care for their dead.

Don't think about it, Daniel. Just do it.

When the stones are in place, I search for a suitable branch to serve as a marker. I prop the branch upright between the stones. Then I close my eyes and say a prayer.

God, if you hear this, please welcome Tony.

I'm as careful going up the cliff as I was coming down. No hurry now. Making sure my feet don't slip, getting a good grip with my hands. A light rain is falling, so that makes it slippery.

Imani peers over the edge, keeping an eye on my progress. She looks worried but doesn't say anything, so as not to make me more nervous. At the top, she takes my hand and helps me to level ground.

I expect her to drop my hand, but she doesn't.

"Daniel, that was a good thing you did. A brave thing."

I shrug. Speaking would disturb the lump in my throat.

"Follow me," Imani says, still holding my hand.

Mia is waiting for us in the woods, where she's rigged the blue tarp and is feeding wood to a small campfire.

"Say hello to the boy responsible for Tony's death," she says, her voice tight and angry.

Deacon Bailey has been tied to a tree. His chin is on his chest, and he's crying like a baby.

31.

Make a Promise to Yourself

Mia folds her arms across her chest. "Everything has changed," she announces. "We knew all along our struggle was dangerous, and now the worst has happened. The question is, what do we do about it?"

"Tell the police?" I suggest.

"Do you see any police? Sure, once we've been rescued, we tell the police. But until then it's up to us."

"What exactly is up to us?" Imani asks uneasily.

Mia points at Deke. "Does he stay or does he go? Do we leave him tied to the tree and go on our way? Or do we cut him loose, knowing he may attack us again?"

I look at Deke, who appears to be suffering. "Maybe he's learned his lesson."

"Maybe," Mia says, but not like she believes it. "That's what we need to decide. Can he be trusted? It's important that all of us agree. Sort of like a jury examining the evidence."

"That seems fair," Imani says. "Daniel?"

"I guess."

Mia kneels, warming her hands at the campfire. "Before we hold the trial, I have a surprise." She holds out a packet of instant hot chocolate. "I've been saving this for a special time."

I'm ashamed to admit that my mouth waters. I just buried someone I knew. This is no time to celebrate, is it?

"This isn't about celebration," Mia says, as if she's reading my mind. "It's about energy. Hot water, powdered chocolate, and sugar will help us think clearly."

I'm not so sure about that, but am not about to disagree. Mia boils water, adds the packet, and stirs with a stick.

"Careful. Hot hot." She pours cups for Imani and me and herself. And then she pours one more cup.

"Daniel? Do you mind? In case he has a trick up his sleeve, you're the strongest."

"Ha! I seriously doubt that."

Secretly I'm flattered they think I'm strong. I carry the extra cup to where Deke is tied to the tree.

"Dude, do you want some?"

He nods.

"I can't untie you, so you'll have to let me hold the cup."

He nods again.

I've never seen anyone look so miserable as he sips from the cup. Not meeting my eyes, but staring a million miles away. The strange thing is, less than an hour ago I was frightened of Deke, and now I feel sorry for him.

No amount of fame or money would persuade me to trade places with Deacon Bailey. Part of me wants to tell him that, but I don't. Too mean. I'm sick of mean. Mean is what started the war. Mean is what got us here, holding a trial about a dead boy.

Mean sucks, and I want no part of it. Looking at Deke, who is miserable and also the cause of misery, I make a promise to myself. No matter what happens, I will not let myself be cruel to a fellow human being.

32.

Can He Be Trusted?

When the last drop of hot chocolate is gone, Mia rinses our cups in the misty rain. The tarp doesn't extend far enough to cover Deke, but he's not complaining. He's not saying much of anything. Mostly staring at the ground with downcast eyes. He looks so different it's almost scary. One minute he's a strong, confident bully, the next he's shrunk to a hollowed-out version of himself.

Where did the real Deke go? Or is it all an act to gain sympathy?

"So how do we do this?" I ask Mia. "How do we decide what's right?"

She shakes her head, furious at Deke, or maybe furious at the world. "How could you!" she shouts at him. "What were you thinking?"

"Mia?" Imani says, concerned.

Mia takes a deep breath, calms herself. "Okay. We put him on trial. We make our case for why he needs to stay tied up, he makes his case for why he should be let go."

"And the three of us have to agree?"

"One way or the other. Yes. Like a real jury." She strides out, hands on her hips, and confronts Deke. "I'll go first, presenting evidence, and then you'll defend yourself. Understood?"

Deke nods grimly.

"Speak up," Mia says. "There can be no misunderstanding. Your life may depend on it."

"Yes. Understood. You first, then me."

Mia retreats from the rain. There's no room to pace under the tarp, but she does the best she can, as if she's ranging around a courtroom, addressing judge and jury. "We charge that it's your fault Tony died. If you hadn't told him to steal the backpack, he'd still be alive."

I've never seen a person look more miserable than Deacon Bailey. Every word from Mia seems to hit him like a punch to the gut.

"What do you say to that?" Mia demands. "Do you deny it?"

He shakes his head. "No, it's true. What happened to Tony is my fault."

"All he wanted to do was be your friend!"

"I know."

"Friends look out for friends! Friends protect friends! They don't let them die showing off! He was trying to impress you, and what did you do to protect him? Nothing!"

"It happened so fast."

124

"We should have been working together, helping each other. All of us! We were stronger together!"

"I was hungry. It made me stupid."

Mia comes charging out from under the tarp. "Are you serious? This isn't about food. That was just the excuse you needed to be a bully! You enjoyed it, lording it over Tony. You enjoyed trying to scare us because you're the biggest and the strongest. You loved it! Admit it!"

Deke shakes his head, his face glistening.

"Admit it!" Mia shouts.

"Okay. You're right," he says. "I don't know why, but it was fun. Stupid, stupid fun."

Mia frowns. "Stupid fun, that's your excuse?"

Deke slumps against the rope. I get the impression he thinks that staging a trial in the middle of the wilderness is a game Mia made up to torment him. But he's wrong. Mia is trying to do the right thing, the best way she knows how.

"What will you do if we untie you? Steal the food? Throw more rocks? We could have been killed!"

That makes him sit up straight and look directly at Mia. "No way! We missed on purpose."

"You expect me to believe that?"

"If I wanted to hurt you, I would have. Maybe I should have. You had all the food!"

"We left a package for you," Mia reminds him. "Six portions. Plus, a pot to boil the water."

"That blew my mind," Deke admits. "Why'd you do it?"

125

"Because it was the right thing to do. Like this is the right thing to do, giving you a chance to defend yourself."

Deke might be crying, or maybe not. Hard to know in the rain.

I feel bad for him, but not so bad I want to see him untied. Because nobody changes that fast. One minute dangerous and violent, the next all sorry for all the rotten things he did. A person like Deacon Bailey can't ever be trusted, can he? Bullies can't change, can they?

"It was all my fault." Deke sounds exhausted, and pleading. "I admit it, okay? Untie me, please. I'll leave you alone, I promise."

He sounds like he means it, but can we trust him with our lives?

33.

What Should I Do?

"What happens next is really important," Mia says to me and Imani, keeping her voice low. "What we decide could make a difference in whether or not we survive. Or Deke survives. If we let him go and he messes with us, we might not make it. Tony made one wrong move and it cost him his life. And if we leave Deke tied to the tree . . ." Her voice trails off.

"Critters with big teeth," I say. "Mountain lions, bears."

"Wolves," Imani says. "I'm pretty sure they have wolves in Montana."

"I can hear you!" Deke shouts, his voice cracking.

Mia marches out to where he's lashed to the tree. "Okay, fine. Your turn. Convince us we should let you go."

He looks up at her, his expression puzzled. "You want me to beg? Okay, I'll beg."

"No begging! Explain why we can trust you."

"Because Tony's dead and I should have saved him and I'm sick of this. Fighting with you guys." He looks angry, but not with us. He's angry at himself.

Mia turns to me and Imani. "Do you believe him?"

I shrug. Imani shakes her head.

"See?" Mia turns back to Deke. "You have to convince us you're not lying. What's changed that will make us believe you?"

"Probably nothing, because you've already decided." He sounds dejected.

"Remember, the verdict has to be unanimous. Convince one of us that you'll stop attacking and we'll set you free."

He stammers, hesitating. "I don't know what to say."

"You told us you enjoyed being a bully. Bullies lie. Bullies can't be trusted."

Deke's head comes up, chin out. "That's what you wanted me to say, so I said it. We were just horsing around, okay? I'm not as bad as you think. I never hit anyone, not hard. Never beat anybody up."

Mia is getting soaked in the drizzling rain, but she pays it no attention. "You called us losers. And that was before the flood. You sneered at all of us. You sneered at the grown-ups who died trying to save us. Every word out of your mouth was dripping with scorn. Like you're the only one in the world who isn't stupid and worthless and beneath your contempt. You threaten us and insist on having every-thing your way. You use your size and strength to intimidate. That's a bully, Deke, look it up."

"Okay. I was a jerk, I did mean things, but I never wanted anybody to die."

Mia nods, as if maybe she believes him. "Explain why you did what you did, and why you won't do it again."

Deke looks baffled. "Did what I did? You mean grab the food?"

Mia is resolute. "Everything. Why you're so cruel. Why you never say a nice thing to anybody. Why you encouraged Tony to make a fool of himself."

"I told you. Because it was fun being big and bad. Stupid fun."

"Deke, that's how everybody sees you. As a big, mean boy! Sorry, but it's the truth. Some people admire bullies, and approve of their behavior, so you probably think you're popular. But you can't really be friends with a bully. Not true friends. Because a bully will turn on you when it becomes convenient."

Deke looks devastated, but maybe he's just feeling sorry for himself. "You'll never trust me, no matter what I say. So what's the point? Take your vote or whatever. Please, let's just get this over with."

He's right. The time has come for making up our minds. Go or stay. Live or die.

Which will it be?

34.

The Gleam in Her Eyes

"You heard him," Mia says. "We have to decide, one way or another. I kept asking Deke to defend himself, to explain why we should trust him, but he never had a good answer."

"Maybe he doesn't know," I say. "People don't always know why they do the things they do. Especially the bad things."

She looks surprised. "Are you defending him?"

"No," I insist. "Just saying."

Imani breaks her silence. "What would happen in a real court, with a real jury?"

"The judge would give them instructions. Then they'd deliberate."

"Deliberating is deciding?"

"Sort of. Deliberate means they examine all the evidence very carefully, and discuss it, and then decide whether the defendant is guilty or not."

"And not guilty is the same as innocent?" I ask.

"No. A guilty verdict means the jury finds the defendant

guilty beyond a reasonable doubt. Not guilty means the evidence wasn't there to convict, but it doesn't mean the defendant is innocent. Innocence is not something that can be proved in court."

"And this isn't a court," Imani says.

"No, it's us deciding what to do. The Team. One for all and all for one. Should we leave him tied up, for our own protection, or let him go?"

"Get it over with!" Deke screams. "Just do it!"

"We're trying to be fair!" Mia shouts back. She turns to us. "I have deliberated and I have decided, so I'll go first. I vote to leave Deacon Bailey tied up. Daniel? Have you made up your mind?"

It's really hard to know what's right or wrong. Sad as it is, I'm not thinking about Tony. He's gone. I'm worried about what Deke might do if we let him loose. I'm worried about losing Mia or Imani. What if he hits them with rocks or shoves them off a cliff? Or me, for that matter. Would he do that, or has he really changed his ways? I don't know, but I'm not sure we can take a chance, even if I have to break my own promise about never being mean to a fellow human being.

I take a deep breath and say, reluctantly, "Convict. Leave him tied to the tree."

Two down, one to go.

"Imani, have you made up your mind?"

Imani lifts her head up, standing tall. There's a kind of

gleam in her eyes I hadn't noticed before. The gleam of a strong person who has something important to say, and is finally getting her chance.

"Cut him loose," she says. "Did you really think I'd leave him to die when this whole miserable trip is my fault?"

Mia, for once, is at a loss for words. And me, I'm just plain stunned. What on earth is Imani talking about?

35.

My Brave Friend

Something about her expression convinces me that Imani is proud of herself for keeping a secret. What secret, exactly, she takes her time revealing. Warming her hands over the fire, clearing her throat, preparing for whatever she's about to say.

"My full name is Imani Walker James. I was signed in to the program as Imani Walker because I didn't want anyone to know my father is Byron James."

Mia's eyes grow as big as saucers. Deke is visibly startled, as well as obviously relieved.

"The new regional middle school exists because of me. This leadership program exists because of me. Not that I wanted either one. It all started two years ago, when I refused to go back to my prep school. I hated it! I hated having security guards. I hated that everybody knew my dad was super wealthy and super famous. Kids acted weird around me, okay? All I wanted was to be treated normal. More than anything, I wanted to go to a public school and just be a regular person."

"Wait," Mia says. "Deke's parents work for Byron James. How come he didn't recognize you?"

Imani shrugs. "Hundreds of people work for my father. Thousands if you count the ones who help build the inventions, or use his patents. Also, my dad has this thing about privacy. He never brings his work home, and he never speaks publicly about family because he's afraid bad things might happen. Like kidnapping, okay? So it was, like, a really big deal when he agreed I could go to public school."

"Your dad invented all kinds of cool stuff! He invented robots!" I exclaim, and then feel embarrassed, because Imani winces, as if she's heard it a million times.

"No, he invents robotic devices. From surgical and medical assistants to driverless cars. And hundreds of other devices. The point is, the only way he'd let me go to a public school is if he built a new one and made sure it had state-of-the-art science labs. I cried about that for a week. I mean, a new school is a great thing, right? But how could I go there if all the kids knew my dad bought the place? That's when my mom suggested using my middle name as my last. Dad would only agree if I promised to go on this white-water thing. He thought it would give me a chance to make friends before the semester starts. I didn't want to go, I personally hate camping because of the bugs and snakes and stuff, but it was the only way. The Project Future Leaders thing in exchange for one year as a normal kid."

134

"Only one year?" I ask.

"It was the most he'd agree to. One year to make real friends, to show other kids who I really am, before they get their minds blown."

"You really hate being your father's kid that much?" I ask.

She flashes me a look that makes me want to melt into the ground. "I love my father! He's totally the best dad in the world! But I hated prep school because so many kids sucked up to me, and some of the parents and teachers, too. All because they wanted to get close to this billionaire celebrity. It's so gross! It made me want to lock myself in my room and hide under the bed. Which is what I did, and how I started this whole mess."

Mia says, "None of this is your fault. You didn't break the dam, or get the grown-ups killed, or make Tony dance on the edge of a slippery cliff."

"No, but if I hadn't wanted to go to public school, we wouldn't be here and none of this would have happened. I'm, like, the worst entitled rich kid that ever lived."

"You're no such thing!" Mia cries, and throws her arms around Imani. "You're my brave friend. Mi amiga brava! And your secret is safe with us. Right, Daniel?"

"Totally!"

To my complete surprise, she turns to Deke. "What about you? Can you keep her secret?"

Without hesitation, he says, "Of course. Are you kidding?

135

If I told, my parents would probably get fired. So, does this mean you'll let me go?"

Mia borrows my jackknife and opens the blade as she approaches the prisoner.

"Not exactly," she says. "Did you think we're stupid?"

36.

The Invisible Rope

Mia uses the blade to cut a length of rope. She wraps it around Deke's hands and wrists and ties it, not too tight and not too loose.

"I thought you were letting me go," he protests.

"We're bringing you with us. You'll hike with us, drink with us, eat with us, rest with us. Share whatever danger we might run into. But the ropes stay until you show you can be trusted."

"Ropes?"

Mia cuts away the rope that holds him to the tree, but leaves a length around his waist. There's an extra ten feet or so. She hands it to me.

"Your new job, Daniel. Keep hold of the rope. If he tries to run, or attack any of us, trip him up."

Deke doesn't look happy about his new situation. "I'm not going to do any of those things. I gave my word."

Mia looks at me and Imani. "Should we tell him?"

I shrug. Why not? Imani nods her okay.

"We made a pact, the three of us. A friends-forever

pact. We call ourselves the Dream Team because we like the sound of it. Also because that was the name of an Olympic basketball team. Imani's dad is a big fan and that's what gave her the idea. It means we've got each other's backs, no matter what."

Deke has this look, very still, almost blank. Like he doesn't want anybody to know what he's thinking. "I get it," he says. "Friends forever. The Dream Team. That's cool."

Is he sneering at us, or is he envious? Impossible to tell.

We pack away the tarp and prepare to go, even though the sun will be setting soon enough. Like staying near the scene of the accident would be bad luck, or make us feel spooky about the body in the ravine. Better to hike in the rain for a while, and put a few miles between us.

When Imani suggests we get moving, Deke tugs on his rope.

"Let me near the edge. There's something I want to say."

Mia shrugs, *Why not?* but gives me a look that says, *Be careful.*

I stop Deke a few feet from the edge. Last thing we need is another accident. He looks down at the mound of stones covering the body. He places his roped-up hands over his heart, and with a strong voice shouts, "Sorry, Tony! Sorry! Sorry! I'm so sorry! I should have protected you!"

He turns away from the cliff, shaking his head. The sadness in his eyes looks real to me.

138

"Wait," Mia says. "He's right. We need to say a few words."

We gather at the edge, although not as close as Deke went.

"What do we say?" It makes me feel stupid having to ask, but I've never been to a funeral.

Mia shakes her head, embarrassed. "I don't know. But something. Imani, any ideas?"

Imani nods firmly. "We should say a prayer."

We bow our heads.

"God, we want you to know that Anthony Meeks wasn't bad, not in his heart. He did stupid things sometimes, but please forgive him. We do. We forgive him. Amen."

"Amen," we echo.

We trudge along the river for an hour and then make camp. Rigging the tarp, making a fire, boiling water, sharing a meal. There's not much talk, and no joking around. We can feel him back there, under the stones, tugging at us with an invisible rope. Reminding us what happened. Asking us, without words, that we never forget him.

We never do.

Day Six

37.

Between a Scream and a Crying-Out

The next morning, things change. Not only that we're escorting a prisoner. The river itself is changing, straightening itself out. The curves are no longer tight and crazy. The high ravine walls get lower and lower until finally we're hiking at river level, with a forest of aspen trees running right up to the water's edge.

And the rain has stopped, at least for now. The clouds remain low and dark, with tendrils of mist that reach almost to the ground. It's a great relief not to be showered on, or drizzled on, or pelted by a downpour. We're all feeling better, excited to think that our rescue might be around the next slow bend.

Mia is in an especially good mood. "When we get back, I'm never eating freeze-dried anything ever again. Everything fresh!"

"Know what I miss most?" Imani says. "Breakfast cereal with cold milk. Honey Nut Cheerios, they rock the bowl."

"Cinnamon Toast Crunch!" Just the words make my mouth water.

"What about you, Deke? What food do you miss?"

He keeps trudging along, not saying a word. I have to hurry to keep up with him.

"Deke? Earth to Deke?"

He turns to look at Imani. "Don't pretend you care. I'll be a good little boy, I won't fight the rope. But we all know that when we get back home, you're going to tell everyone that Tony was my fault. I'm the bad guy, you're the heroes. That's your story."

Mia says, "Deke? Take a chill pill. We might surprise you."

"Whatever. Let's get rescued. Let's get this over with." He charges ahead, dragging me along.

We cover a couple of miles like that, before Deke stops to drink from the river. A few minutes go by before Mia and Imani catch up. But it's not like Deke is trying to escape. Like he says, he's in a hurry to get it over with, whatever shame or punishment is coming his way.

The way he's acting, sneering at himself, I'm pretty sure he thinks he deserves it.

I ask myself again, *Can a bully change?*

Later in the afternoon, the river changes again. It gets narrow and fast, and we can hear rapids in the distance. The riverbanks we've been hiking along have been clean for miles, but now we're coming upon places where

144

broken trees have been driven ashore. Evidence of the busted dam, and a pain for us, because we have to find a way around the piles of debris, and that takes extra time and effort.

For me it's a painful reminder of that terrible night. The earth-shaking roar of the dam destroyed, and the killing flood that followed. The night that changed everything. One minute, we were kids with grown-ups in charge, monitoring and guiding our every move. The next minute, we had to figure it out for ourselves. Lost in the rain, and lost in other ways, too. Making choices and decisions no kid should ever have to make.

So much for a good mood. Reliving that night makes me long for home, for a wonderful memory that happened just before I left for the white-water trip. The Fourth of July was a fantastic day, with a cookout and fireworks and games and stuff. Best of all, everybody was doing great, especially Dad, who has a new job designing websites. Okay, everybody was doing great except my brother Phil, who was so worried about mountain lions getting me that it gave him tummy problems. That's when we looked it up together, how to survive an attack, and I told him not to worry, I'd be home soon.

It hurts that my little brothers must be worried sick, not to mention Mom and Dad. I picture myself walking through the front door of our house, unannounced. How shocked and happy they'll be to see me. That should make me happy, but instead I feel like crying. I'm so homesick it hurts in my guts and all over.

"Did you hear that?" Deke says. "Is that a helicopter?"

We search the leaden sky, the clouds so low they touch the trees.

"Sorry, I'm pretty sure that's the sound of the rapids."

"No," he insists, his expression furiously intense. "Not a helicopter. I was wrong. This is higher, and very faint."

We listen, hear nothing out of the ordinary. Is this some trick Deke is hatching? Distracting us with imaginary noises while he makes a break for it?

Suddenly he's yanking on the rope, dragging me along. "Up ahead. I'm sure of it."

Mia and Imani struggle to keep up. We're making our own noise, scrambling over piles of busted trees, which makes it even harder to hear. But as Deke urges us along, I start to believe him.

A high-pitched sound, coming and going. A noise both familiar and terrifying. Somewhere between a scream and a crying-out.

We all hear it at the same time, and stop in our tracks.

"Help! Help! HELP!"

The hair lifts on the back of my neck. A woman's voice, crying for help.

38.

The Most Dangerous Thing

"Hush!" Deke says.

He turns in a slow circle, trying to determine where the cry for help came from. It hasn't been repeated, at least not in the last minute or so. Was it something we imagined? Something we wanted to hear so bad that we mistook the cry of a bird?

No. It was real.

"Whoever it is, she's probably injured. Maybe she passed out. We have to find her." Deke holds out his hands. "Untie me so I can help. You want to find out if I can be trusted? Here's your chance."

Another noise or sound. Not a cry, but a faint whimper. Somewhere close.

Mia says, "Fine! Daniel?"

I take out my jackknife, open the blade, and cut the rope from his wrists. Instantly he runs to a debris pile and starts pulling aside broken branches. "Hey! We're here! Make a noise and we'll find you!"

But there are no more sounds. No cries for help. No

147

whimpers. Deke, frantic, gets all the way to the bottom of that debris pile. Nothing there but busted trees and some small boulders from the flood.

"She has to be here!" Deke cries out. "Make a noise! Please make a noise!"

Silence.

Imani speaks quietly. "Sound carries over the water. It can fool you, right? You think something is close, but it's not."

Deke is frustrated. "What are you saying?"

"Maybe that cry for help came from the other side of the river." She points. "There's flood stuff over there, too."

She's right, at least about the debris piles on the opposite shore. But how to get there with no raft?

"Rope," Deke says. "Tie the rope to my waist."

"But we just cut it loose," Mia says impatiently.

"Just do it. We need to hurry. Nobody else dies, not today."

We retie the rope to his waist, and add another full coil of rope from the backpack. The river has narrowed to maybe fifty yards across, but the current has increased. Deke picks his spot and slogs into the water, standing strong against the current.

"Shallow here!" he shouts. "I can make it!"

Mia and I secure the rope, letting it out as he advances. Imani is on the riverbank, ready to jump in if necessary. She claims she's a strong swimmer and has passed a lifeguard rescue test. Deke is right about the shallow area—the water never gets more than waist deep. He slips once or twice, but always regains his footing.

Before long, he clambers onto the opposite riverbank and shakes himself like a dog. "Come on over, the water's fine!" he shouts. "I've got this end of the rope! I need your help to find her! Please!"

The three of us take a vote. Cross the river or not? "This is the most dangerous thing we've done since the raft," Mia reminds us.

"We have to do it," Imani insists. "A life may depend on it."

"Daniel?"

"I say we go for it."

"It means trusting Deke with the other end of the rope."

"I know. I do trust him, at least about this."

We put our hands together, and make our pledge. "All agreed! One for all, all for one!"

Ten minutes later, we're all safely across. Soaked to the skin, chilled by the powerful current, but safe on the other side.

Deke is eager to get to work. "Dan! Grab the other end and lift! I heard somebody under there, I swear!"

I take hold of a large tree branch, and put my shoulder under it. I lift with all my strength while Deke does the same thing at the other end. Slowly the big branch rises, bringing with it a mass of wet leaves.

"There! I see her!" Deke shouts. "Pull her out while we hold this up! Hurry! Careful! Careful! She's badly hurt!"

Deke and I hold the branch up, our knees trembling with effort. Imani and Mia duck beneath the branch, and then, ever so carefully, they drag out a frail and broken body, and carry her clear of the leaves under which she'd been hidden.

Cindi Beacon. Soccer star Cindi, who helped save us, who was swept away by the flood.

She's alive!

39.

A Better Idea

Cindi is alive but badly injured. We can't tell for sure, but it looks like she has broken bones in every limb. Probably broken ribs, too, because she can't take a deep breath without crying out in pain.

I'm frantic to help her but don't know where to begin. Imani is the calm one, gently touching her fingers to Cindi's wrist, and bending low to hear what she has to say. Her voice is weak, little more than a whisper.

"She wants to know if Sky and Tony are okay," Imani says.

Mia's face falls. She shakes her head and says, "We're sorry to have to tell you this, Cindi, but they didn't make it."

Good answer. That's all she needs to know right now.

Imani listens as Cindi tries to speak, her voice barely a whisper.

"She doesn't remember the flood," Imani tells us. "The only thing she remembers is waking up under this tree, and drinking rainwater from the leaves. Then hearing

151

voices—us—and using all her strength to cry out. She thought she was dreaming, but she had to try."

"Tell her she saved us. Without her we'd never have made it up that cliff."

"You just told her yourself," says Imani with a tense smile. "Her hearing is okay, but she's very weak. She needs water immediately. And, Mia, can we prepare a meal? She has to be starving even if she doesn't feel hungry."

"Of course!"

Mia shrugs off her backpack, retrieving the essentials. Deke and I search for dry wood and kindling. He hasn't had much to say since we found Cindi, but his eyes are troubled.

"You saved her. Feel good about it."

"What if she dies?" he whispers, not wanting her to hear us.

"We won't let that happen."

"You can't know what will happen, Daniel. None of us can."

He's right, of course. Here I am trying to cheer him up, and he points out that I'm full of baloney. Somehow, it's not an insult, it's stating the truth. The fact that Cindi Beacon survived the flood is a miracle, but it doesn't mean we know how to keep her alive. She needs EMTs, not a handful of sixth graders. That will only come with a rescue.

Where are they? Why haven't they found us?

Deke notices me searching the empty sky. "They must think we're dead, that nothing could have survived the dam breaking."

"Nobody knew we were rafting the Crazy," I point out.

Deke shrugs. "It doesn't matter why they haven't found us. What matters is we're on our own. We can't assume we'll be rescued. I thought so at first, but I was wrong."

I point out that he was the one who was so sure we'd be found in a day or two that there was no reason to ration the food.

"I was an idiot," he says contemptuously. "I thought it was all a game."

We've gotten good at building fires, and soon the water is boiling and Mia is making a meal. One of the last few. She adds extra water to make a broth for Cindi, because that will be easier to swallow. Imani helps her get down a cup, and the effort makes her so exhausted that she falls asleep.

Imani joins us at the fire, and keeps her voice low. "I'm no expert, but her pulse seems weak. She needs to be in a hospital."

"Two choices." Mia sounds fierce and determined. "Stay here, take care of her as best we can, and hope to be rescued. Or bring her with us."

"How can we move her without making it worse? She hurts so bad."

"Good point. Maybe staying is the best way to help her."

153

"No. No. No." It takes enormous effort for Cindi to make herself heard. She strains to lift her head, pleading with us. "Bring me with you. Please. If we stay here, I'll die."

Her request can't be refused, not after what she sacrificed for us. The question is how best to move her. Mia suggests we find broken branches and make some sort of stretcher. But are we strong enough to lift her? Can we keep it up for miles?

"Stretcher won't work," Deke announces. "Too awkward on these paths."

"Got a better idea?"

"I'll carry her," he says. "We stay together and we keep moving."

40.

Not a Good Sign

It's amazing how useful a piece of blue tarp can be. Imani and Mia rig it into a carrier for Cindi. Like an adult version of a baby carrier that Deke can slip over his shoulders. At Cindi's suggestion, they tie her legs together so they won't flop around.

Tiny Dancer makes sense as a nickname. I doubt she weighs a hundred pounds. Even so, Deke is the only one big enough and strong enough to carry her.

"Once we start, I'm going to let myself pass out," she says in her whispery weak voice. "Please don't worry. I'm not dying. It's my way of coping with the pain."

Poor Cindi. I feel so bad for her it makes me want to cry. But I don't, because that would make things worse. We're trying to be cheerful and hopeful for her sake. No idea how long it will take to finish the hike, find the pickup location, and get her the help she needs. But we'll do our best.

Our mission has expanded. We not only strive to save ourselves, we do whatever it takes to save Cindi Beacon.

She's our hero. That terrible night is burned into my brain. I can still see it, feel it, taste the fear. And I'll never forget the look on Cindi's face as she pushed Imani up onto the cliff. She assumed she was about to die, and the last thing she did was save a child rather than herself. She was terrified, but she did the right thing anyway.

That has to be the true definition of courage.

"Ready?" Mia asks. "I'll go first and make sure the path is clear. Daniel and Imani, you follow Deke and help him if he loses balance."

Deke takes a deep breath, braces himself. "Let's do it."

True to her word, Cindi passes out before he's taken three steps. Best thing, I guess. Not that I can imagine how much it must hurt.

"You okay, Deke?"

His expression is grim and determined. "Got it. No worries, I can do this all day."

If I had to carry a hundred pounds on my back, I'd keel over for sure. But Deacon Bailey keeps pace with Mia as if it really isn't a problem.

Imani pays close attention to the unconscious Cindi, makes sure she's still breathing. I'm watching Deke's legs and feet, ready to prop him up if he loses balance. Nobody talks much, nobody sings. We're focused on our mission.

Despite being scared that we'll fail, I feel better than I have since that first night on the beach, before the flood.

156

We're doing the right thing, working together to help someone else, and it feels good. That makes me stronger, more confident. Is it possible that getting picked for the leadership program wasn't a mistake? Did some adult see something in me I didn't know I had?

Daniel Redmayne, born leader. Ha!

"What's so funny?" Imani asks as we hike along, bringing up the rear.

"Nothing. Just thinking."

"About what?"

"I never thought I could do stuff like this."

"Like what?"

"Survive in the wilderness."

She grins. "Me neither. Maybe my father had the right idea. Not that he wanted terrible things to happen, or people to die! Just the part about me being on my own, and speaking up for myself, and making friends. That part has been good."

The ground beside the river gets steeper and trickier as the Crazy dips through a series of rapids. Then it levels out for a while, and the river widens. All the while, Deke remains sure-footed and strong. He refuses to take a break. "She's getting weaker. I can feel it. We have to keep going."

"Oh no!" exclaims Mia, who is out ahead by ten yards or so.

I catch up to her. "What's wrong?"

Then I see what has her spooked. A black bear with its front paws in the river. It stares at us with glittering black eyes, snorting and shaking its head from side to side.

Not a good sign. Not a good sign at all.

41.

Never Play Dead

"What do we do?"

They're asking me because of what I did with the mountain lion. "I'm not sure. Off the top of my head, all I really know about bears is you're not supposed to run. Or get between a mother and her cubs."

The bear starts making a huffing noise. *Oof! Oof! Oof!* It sounds ticked off, angry. And it shuffles around, directly facing us from about thirty yards away.

"Give me a hand! Quick!" Deke needs help lowering Cindi to the ground.

"What are you going to do?"

"I don't know. Something. The three of you keep her safe!"

Before I can think to stop him, he slips around Mia and takes a position between her and the bear. He raises his hands over his head, making himself as tall as possible, like we did with the mountain lion.

"Go away!" he shouts. "Leave us alone!"

The bear responds by standing up on its hind legs

and baring its fangs. Making itself taller than Deke.

"Not good, Deke! Be careful!"

I'm racking my brain, trying to remember what little I know about bears. Black bears like we have in New Hampshire. I've seen a few, but never close up. And never standing on hind legs to full height. Looking plenty dangerous, with dripping fangs and claws displayed.

Mia, Imani, and I stand guard over Cindi, who is moaning but not fully conscious. I doubt she knows what's going on. We link our arms, forming a human wall to protect her.

"Go away!" Deke shouts, his voice booming. "Get!"

The bear waddles closer on hind legs, front paws scratching the air.

"Deke! I just remembered something! If it attacks, fight back! Don't play dead! Never play dead!"

I'm not sure he hears what I'm saying, he's so focused on standing up to the bear, not backing down. His hands are fists. His chest is pumped out, and the muscles on his shoulders and neck are tensed. He looks plenty scary to me, but the bear doesn't seem to be impressed. It advances another step, spittle pouring from its open mouth.

Deke stops shouting words and makes a roaring scream. A human growl.

The bear responds by dropping to the ground. It scratches at the ground to show the power of its claws.

And then it puts its head down and charges straight at Deke.

I'm pretty sure that if it was me standing there, I'd have cut and run. Tried to climb a tree, or maybe jump in the river, even though I know a bear can't be outrun or out-climbed. But not Deke. He doesn't move an inch. Bears look kind of slow and ambling when they're walking around sniffing at stuff, but when they charge, the speed is unreal. This bear comes at Deke like it's been shot from a cannon. It crashes into Deke's legs, sending him head over heels to the ground.

The bear skids to a stop just in time to see Deke leap to his feet, pumping his fists over his head. For some reason, that freaks the bear out. It moans, head shaking from side to side, as if unable to decide what to do next.

Then it bolts into the woods, as if running for its life, and vanishes into the trees.

We're safe!

"Deke!"

He's down on the ground, with both hands around the lower part of his right leg. Holding tight as blood gushes from between his fingers.

42.

Look Up at the Stars

Mia digs into the pack and retrieves the first aid kid. Deke is the one who is wounded, but it's me who feels woozy from the sight of blood. A little of my own, like scraping a knee, that's okay. But someone else? All I can do not to barf.

Imani takes charge because she's passed a CPR course. She examines the wound on his calf. "Not too deep."

"Deep enough to cut me." Deke sounds grumpy. Who could blame him?

"Sorry. Looks like three claws grazed you on the way by. I'm going to open one of these antiseptic wipes, and then we'll bandage you up."

"Fine. Thanks."

"This will sting," Imani says apologetically.

Deke grimaces, but doesn't moan or cry out. He may not be acting like a bully right at the moment, but he's still tough as nails. As soon as the bandage is taped to his calf, he gets to his feet and picks up Cindi's carrier by the shoulder straps. "We need to keep moving."

162

"Sure you don't need a break?"

"I want to put some distance between us and the bear."

Good idea. Great idea. Do bears return to the scene of a confrontation? No idea, and no interest in finding out.

We tramp along the river until the sun gets low in the sky. All of us disappointed that we haven't reached the pickup location by the end of the day, or been found by rescuers. And worried sick because Cindi is getting worse. Mostly she's out of it, muttering about stuff that doesn't make any sense. Imani says it's called delirium.

"It happens when you're in shock, and I think she's been in shock since the flood. She must have a really strong heart or she'd be gone by now."

"We'll make a fire, keep her warm. See if she'll swallow some broth."

Deke and I are on kindling detail. He's limping a little and trying to hide it.

"That was a brave thing you did."

He snorts. "Didn't feel brave. Felt stupid."

"Whatever, it worked. You got rid of the bear."

"Next time I'm jumping in the river."

"Bears can swim," I remind him.

"So can I."

I get the impression he doesn't want to talk about it, so I stop pushing. But I'm wondering about bullies. Who they are and why they act so mean. Have they been bullied, too, or do they just enjoy it? Can they change? Or are they bullies for life? The sneering part of Deke still shows, but he's mostly sneering at himself, and he hasn't said anything cruel since Tony fell from the cliff.

I'm starting to think it isn't an act, that this is the real Deke Bailey. He had this haunted look when the three of us were explaining about being friends for life. Like it was something he wished he could share in, but didn't know how.

When the campfire is going strong, Mia heats up water for our last freeze-dried meal.

"That's it? It's all gone?"

She shakes the bag. "Final ration. But I'm not worried. You want to know why?"

We all do.

"It finally stopped raining. Look up. Those are stars."

We look up, and find ourselves staring into the Milky Way. Billions of stars strewn like jewels across the big Montana sky. I get a lump in my throat. Not sure why. How can something so beautiful make you feel a little sad?

Maybe because it points to the end of our ordeal. Surely, clear skies mean they'll find us. That will be the end of our great and terrible adventure, struggling to survive in the Montana wilderness. Teaching ourselves how to tame the Crazy River. The killing river. Making grown-up decisions and grown-up mistakes. Being given the chance to balance the tragedy by saving one of the adults who tried so hard to help us.

Thinking about it makes me feel out of breath. Or it could be the smoke from the fire.

"Get some rest," Mia says to Deke. "We'll need your strength tomorrow. And maybe your courage."

"Yes, boss."

Mia responds, softly but firmly. "I'm not your boss, Deke. I'm your friend."

I lie down beside the campfire, staring at the embers and trying to slow my mind down so I can sleep. I get this flash, more like a visit in a time machine than an ordinary memory, of Dad tucking me into bed. I was about four years old, and still afraid of sleeping with the lights out. Afraid of things that might be hiding in the dark. I can still feel his hand on my forehead, smoothing my hair away, as he smiled and said there was nothing to be afraid of, and that everyone had nightmares now and then.

"You're in charge of the light," he told me. "If you feel better with it on, leave it on, and don't worry about it. Don't worry about anything."

If only I could do that. Not worry about anything. The sound of the whispering river puts me to sleep.

Day Seven

43.

Big Red

We awake to a perfect blue sky. Hardly any clouds. Cool dry air.

Deke, rigging the carrier to his broad shoulders, is as bright and cheerful as the weather. "Today is the day," he announces. "Byron James will have a fleet of rescue helicopters searching for us, so keep an eye out."

Like he's positive this will be our last day on the trail. I hope he's right, but part of me is more cautious. Go forward hoping for the best, but never forget the danger all around us. Floods, mountain lions, bears. All kinds of creatures out there, capable of inflicting great harm, and the river itself can be deadly. The landscape of steep ravines is awesome, but dangerous. One wrong step, one slip in a bad place, and your life is over.

We know that. And we must not forget, we can never let down our guard.

We head out as before, with Mia picking the trail, clearing the way. Imani and me with Deke, making sure he doesn't get tripped up. The night wasn't good for

169

Cindi. The poor lady moaned and whimpered in her sleep. This morning, she was too weak to swallow a little hot broth that had been saved for her. Her breathing seems really shallow, and even when she's conscious, it's like not all of her is there.

None of us want to say it out loud, but we're scared she's dying.

Imani tries to keep her awake, distracted from her pain. "Hey, Cindi! Cindi Beacon, superstar! Tiny Dancer! You're the best, girl! Tell us about the big game, Cindi! World Cup, so amazing. We'd love to hear all about it. Oh, I know you're hurting. We're going to get the help you need. That's a promise. So, you just hang in there, Cindi! We love you, everybody loves you!"

Cindi briefly opens her glassy eyes. Does she know where she is, or what's going on? I doubt it.

If ever there was a time for a rescue, this is it.

We haven't discussed the actual search that must be going on. But it makes sense a super-wealthy dude like Byron James would spare nothing to locate his missing daughter. He'd be running it like a military operation, hiring planes and helicopters and search parties, like Deke said.

So, where are they? Last thing home base knew about us, we were heading to a river a hundred miles from here. That's where they'd look first. But when they didn't find us at the original destination, they'd widen the search area, right? Would they be looking a hundred miles away? Would they be checking out the remote, Crazy River wilderness? Or was damage from the broken dam so massive they assumed nobody could have survived?

Put that out of your head, Daniel. It doesn't help to imagine the worst, because worst means Cindi Beacon dies before we can find help.

Mia, leading from the front, joins in the optimistic chatter.

"Today is the day. I like the sound of that. First thing when I get back to civilization, wash my hair! Then eat a Big Mac. So icky but so delicious!"

Imani joins in. "I agree with the icky part! First thing the same for me, wash my hair for sure. Clean clothes. Then a cold, cold glass of milk. Then change into my favorite jammies and go to bed and let my mom read stories to me like she did when I was little."

"Daniel?"

"I'm gonna roll in the dirt like a dog, because I'm still not dirty enough. Arf!"

That cracks the girls up.

"That's so funny, Daniel! Deke, what about you?" Mia asks.

Silence for a few yards. Then, "I'd rather not think about it."

Meaning he *is* thinking about it. What to tell Tony Meeks's family. *Sorry, your son died trying to impress me.*

171

That shuts us up for a while. The reminder that even though we left Tony behind, he's still with us. It's such a big thing, his death and what to do about it. Like an extra weight we're carrying around.

Ahead, Mia gasps and points. "¡Dios mío! I don't believe it!"

We all see it. On the shore and fully inflated, a big red raft.

44.

The Big Hush

The raft is the same one that carried us through white water on the very first day. Astonishing that it survived the flood without any obvious damage. Sky Hanson's Wild River Adventures, stamped on the front, reminds us of who we've lost. At the same time, it's like a gift from Sky. He can't be there to help us, so his raft will have to do.

No life jackets—they had been hung up to dry and must have been swept away—but two paddles remain, firmly strapped inside the raft. Four paddles would be better, but two will do.

We drag the raft into the water, leaving it tethered to a tree while we transfer Cindi. Lowering her ever so carefully into the middle, between the inflated seats. She groans and her eyes flutter. Not all-the-way conscious, but aware of what's happening.

A smile forms on her lips, then she's deep asleep. Still breathing, but just barely.

"Hang on, Cindi. Help is on the way, or we're on the

173

way to help. Soon. We promise. We love you, Cindi, please stay with us."

We're hoping that the next time she wakes up will be when she's loaded into an ambulance. Until then we'll do all we can to keep her safe and alive.

"We need a plan," Deke says. "What do we do if we get to some rapids? I'm worried she won't survive getting banged around in white water. Or thrown from the raft without a life jacket."

Mia agrees. "We'll be extra careful. If the current picks up, or we hear rapids, Imani and I will make sure she's secure. You and Daniel take the paddles. Agreed?"

"Sounds good. Agreed."

"We'll need to stay as much in the middle of the river as possible. Can't risk being thrown ashore."

"Got it. Piece of cake."

"Don't say 'cake.' I'm starved."

We're kidding around because we're all nervous. Our last white-water adventure, with the raft made of logs, was a disaster. On the other hand, if Sky's raft made it through the flood, a wall of water thirty feet high, it can survive just about anything.

Deke and I man the paddles, but we don't have to do much except steer now and then. The water remains calm, carrying us smoothly downriver at a mile or two an hour. The sun is out, the sky is clear, and we're passing through some of the most beautiful wilderness in the world.

As we come around a long slow curve, a moose clomps out of the forest and lowers her head into the water, drinking deeply. I recognize the animal because we have them in New Hampshire. Believe me, you don't want to get in a car wreck with a moose! They can weigh over a thousand pounds. This one is female—no antlers—and as we pass by, her two calves join her at the water's edge. Mom and kids.

"That's so cute," Mia says.

"That's the first big creature we've seen that hasn't wanted to kill us," Deke points out.

Imani laughs. "Don't say that too loud. Moose can swim."

Momma moose watches us drift by. We're not the first rafters she's ever seen, and she knows we're no threat. A little while later, a huge bald eagle swoops over the water, reaches down with its talons, and snags a fish. Amazing. It's like Montana is showing off. *Look at me, I am magnificent!*

We're distracted from the scenery by Cindi trying to speak. Or is she choking? Imani holds Cindi's head up and pours a little water over her cracked lips. That's what she wanted, something to drink.

"That's a good sign, isn't it?" I ask. "She hasn't given up."

Imani looks so serious it gives me the chills. "Hope we get there soon. I'm starting to think it doesn't exist, this pickup location connected to a road."

"Has to be real," says Mia fiercely. "Sky told us,

remember? We'd put in by the dam, and there would be another van waiting at the end of the adventure."

"I wasn't really paying attention," I admit. "Funny how you don't pay attention, and later it turns out to be a matter of life and death."

"We'll find it. There will be a road, and we'll flag down the first vehicle we see. They'll help us. They have to!"

We're starting to feel panicky, me most of all, because it was my idea to go downriver, rather than wait to be rescued. Maybe I was wrong. Maybe we should have stayed where we were, waiting for the rain to stop and the sky to clear.

Suddenly, Deke perks up, lifting his head. "Hear that? Get ready."

I grip the paddle with all my might. The river picks up speed, and the familiar sound gets louder and louder. *SSSSSSSSSSSSSSSSSHHHHHHHHHHHHH.*

Soon it will be roaring. The big hush of white water.

45.

The Most Beautiful Sound on Earth

Mia and Imani drape themselves over the inflatable seats and grab the handholds. Locking themselves into position over Cindi, acting as her human shields, so she can't be tossed out.

They look so determined that it inspires me to be better than I am. No matter how much it scares me, I'll do my best. I'll rise above.

"Get ready!" Deke shouts. "Here it comes!"

I'm on one side, armed with a paddle, he's on the other. We're going to keep this raft upright in the middle of the river. Cindi Beacon isn't dying on our watch, no matter how rough the rapids. Bring it on, you crazy river!

And it does. The hush becomes a roar, and suddenly we're in it, waves breaking over the sides. In that first moment, I'm drenched and blinded, my glasses so wet I can't see anything clearly.

"Deke! Can't see! Tell me what to do!"

"Okay! Wait, wait! Now! Go!"

I plunge the paddle deep and pull with all my might. One stroke, two.

"Stop! Wait! Go!"

Five more strokes, straining every muscle in my body. Ripping along with the white water is like riding a toboggan down a bumpy slope, only softer. I hope Cindi has passed out, because every twist and jounce must hurt. The raft is amazingly buoyant. No matter how steep the wave, it bounces back on top. Thanks to Sky Hanson for buying the best gear, and for teaching us the basics.

"Boulder dead ahead!" Deke screams. "GO! GO! GO!"

I'm battling blind, eyes stinging. Concentrating on keeping hold of the paddle, because without it we'd be lost. The water keeps trying to wrench it away, but I'd rather die than let go.

WHAM!

The raft slams into the side of the boulder. We spin in a circle, facing backward as the current rips us away.

"GO! GO!"

Straining to paddle as hard as possible and not fall out of the raft.

"STOP!"

With one hand, I clear my glasses enough so I can see we're facing forward, and remain in the middle of the river. Then we're thumping in steep shallows, barely clearing the rocky bottom. Mist rises from the turbulence like steam, making it difficult for either of us to see what lies ahead.

How long can this go on? Can poor Cindi survive the violent movements of the raft, which is being flung about like a beach ball in the surf?

"Almost clear! Hang on!"

We spin again, out of control. What did he mean, almost clear? Did we barely miss another rock?

The raft pitches forward—backward for us—and the bow area is submerged for a second before popping back up. Water swirls around my legs.

"Help her!" I scream. "She'll drown!"

The girls assure me she's okay, that the area between the inflatable seats did not flood. The current begins to slow and then we're out of the rapids and back into calm water. I kneel on the paddle to keep it from getting loose and wipe my glasses with my shirt. Deke looks like a big wet dog, totally soaked, but the look in his eyes warns me not to make any wise remarks. Not that I would dare.

"She's awake!" Mia sounds greatly relieved. "Cindi says to thank you. She says we are her guardian angels."

I'm shaking from the chill of the water. Also from sheer exhaustion. That was like ten of the gym class workouts I always hated. Other kids could do like twenty pull-ups. I couldn't even do one. But somehow I paddled hard enough to keep up with big strong Deke, and we all came through alive.

I'm so tired I want to curl up and sleep, but my heart is pounding way too hard. If we come upon another stretch

179

of white water, we're doomed, because my skinny arms feel like they're about to fall off. I look over at Deke and realize he's as exhausted as I am. But not so tired he can't give me a high five. "You did good, dude. I could barely keep up."

That can't be true, but it's nice to hear.

wuppa

"What's that?" Imani sounds awestruck. "DO YOU HEAR THAT?"

wuppa wuppa

Oh yes, we all hear it, even Cindi, who lifts her head and stares into the sky with a smile on her face and her eyes beaming. We're listening to the most beautiful sound on earth.

wuppa wuppa wuppa

Helicopter blades.

46.

Something We Need to Discuss

My brain is shouting, *WOW WOW WOW*, but I can't seem to say it out loud. Too choked up. Doesn't matter, Mia is cheering for all of us. She stands up in the tippy raft, waving both arms at the big orange helicopter hovering over us.

"We did it! We did it! I can't believe it, we actually DID IT!"

A helmeted crewman leans out of the open door of the helicopter and points to the shore. Both sides of the river are heavily forested, so there's no place to land. The rescue will take place from the air.

Deke and I don't have to discuss it, we know what to do. Dig in with our paddles and get to the shore, fast as possible.

Imani leaps out, takes the rope, and ties it to a tree.

"Cindi first!" she shouts, but of course she can't be heard above the roar of the helicopter. It hovers directly overhead. The downdraft from the blades roars like a hurricane, knocking leaves and small branches from

181

the shivering aspen trees, spreading white rings in the water.

The noise is overwhelming. Imani and Mia make themselves understood by pointing at Cindi, lying between the inflatable seats, and holding up one finger. First, take her first! The crewman leaning out of the helicopter gives a thumbs-up. A rescue cradle is slowly lowered. Imani and I grab the ends, positioning it next to the raft while Deke gently lifts Cindi from between the seats.

She's awake, although unable to speak above the roar of the blades. Deke places her in the cradle, and we fasten the safety straps. After we back away, the cradle rises, slowly turning a graceful pirouette as they pull it into the helicopter. Once she's inside, the guy in the helmet leans out and somehow makes us understand that we should stay where we are and they'll return for us. Cindi Beacon, the Tiny Dancer who scored that amazing goal, will soon be on her way to the closest trauma center.

That's what Mia meant by "We did it." We saved her by working together, and by not giving up. We can be proud of that for the rest of our lives. Maybe that will balance out the shameful events that also happened.

The big orange helicopter speeds away, and as we wait for it to return, Mia wipes the tears from her eyes and reaches out. "Take hands! You too, Deke. The Dream Team has something to discuss. It's about Tony."

A discussion takes place, about what to tell his family. We make a pledge to Tony, and a vow to ourselves. Four brave friends holding hands in the wilderness, having survived for seven long days.

I couldn't be more proud of them, and of myself.

47.

It's So Good to Be Alive

I'd tell you about our own rescue, how we all went up in the same cage, but it turns out helicopters and I don't get along. I puked and I puked, three bags full. Well, not quite, but that's how it felt, heaving on an empty stomach. Too busy being sick to pay much attention to the flight, or what we could see out the open door. Just the sight of an open door and *What if we fall out?* was enough to turn me into a barf-o'-matic machine.

I do know they flew us to the same hospital in Missoula where Cindi Beacon was being treated. That we landed on a helipad and were guided inside. That the rescue crew turned us over to a medical crew before we could properly thank them.

Within a few minutes, I feel way better.

"Daniel Redmayne?" The super-nice lady escorting me checks off my name. "The docs will need to give you a thorough checkup, make sure you're good to go, but first there's somebody who wants to see you. A lot of somebodies."

They're waiting for me in the ER lobby. My family. All of them. My little brothers, Philip, Jon, and Mark. My mom, of course, she's always there for us. And, yes, my father, too. He looks shaky and trembles a little from his medication, like always, but he's beaming like the sun.

My brothers swarm me, grabbing hold of my arms and legs as if to assure themselves that I'm really there.

Is it possible to weep gleefully? Yes.

"We knew! We knew you'd be okay! Were there lions? Were there bears?"

"Both!"

"Tell us! Tell us!"

"Maybe later. I promise. Let me hug Mom, okay?"

I never knew Mom was so strong. She practically cracks my ribs as she nuzzles my hair and strokes my face. "My baby boy, all grown up."

Dad is the last to embrace me. Keeping my voice down, I ask if he's okay.

He nods. "The illness remains. There's no cure, I just have to deal with it. When they told us you were missing, I assumed I'd fall to pieces. Somehow that didn't happen."

"That's great, Dad."

"I'm not saying I'll never need help again, but for now I'm good."

Everybody is making a fuss, pointing out that I'm skinnier than ever, but I don't mind. It may change later, when things get back to normal, but for right now, I love everything about my family, and everything about my life.

It's so good to be alive.

The physical examination takes a lot longer than I expected. No, they didn't count my freckles, but they checked everything else, from heart rate to lung capacity.

"Healthy as a horse," says the doc who finally signs me out. "Good to go, young man. The staff wants to thank you and your friends for what you did for Ms. Beacon. Have no doubt, without your efforts she would not be alive."

There's that to feel good about. On the downside, cadaver dogs are out searching the Crazy for the remains of Sky Hanson. It's possible his body has been buried under so much flood debris that it will never be found, but we owe it to him to try.

Tony's body has already been recovered, thanks to the helicopter crews, who spotted the primitive grave marker we left behind. His family will be able to give him a real funeral and bury him properly.

I get it that bad things happen to good people, that life can be dangerous when you least expect it. But that doesn't mean I have to like it.

All four of the survivors' families have a reunion at the airport that includes ice cream and hamburgers and guess what? WE GET TO FLY BACK ON BYRON JAMES'S CORPORATE JET!

He turns out to be a really awesome dude, wicked smart of course, and Imani's mother is so nice and regular acting, not fancy rich at all. She thanks all of us for never giving up. "I'm so sorry to hear about your friend Tony."

It's so sad and tragic that we can't bear to think about it. But we can't *not* think about it, so there it is, the Tony thing, never going away.

Mia catches my eye and nods. She gets it. Imani, too.

Deke, seated with his mom and dad, looks happy enough at first glance. He's got a lot to deal with, but he'll be okay. Because he has three forever friends, amigos bravos, and we'll never let him down.

As for me, for the first time in my life, I'm looking forward to getting back to school. I'm going to take an art class, also for the first time, because if I'm going to write a graphic novel about my dad and how he deals with his condition, I need to improve my drawing skills.

If you're going to be a good writer, you have to take it seriously, you have to be fully committed, no matter what. You have to understand that nothing is guaranteed, that things can go wrong. Mistakes get made, accidents can happen. And you can't let that stop you.

Like I learned on the Crazy River, there are times that even if something is super scary, you just have to go all in.

Thirty Days Later

The four of us are up in the bleachers of the Sky Hanson Gymnasium, witnessing the dedication ceremony for the brand-new Byron James Regional Middle School. It's quite a spectacle. Cindi Beacon wanted to be there, but is about to enter a long-term rehab facility. She misses a short speech by Byron James himself, and an appearance by the New Hampshire governor, who presents the famous inventor with a "key to the state."

"You shared your imagination with the world, and now, lucky for us, you're sharing your fortune!"

That gets a lot of laughs. Imani goes along with it, but I'm sure she feels the weight of it, all that fame and money. We're our own tribe now, and we're tight. We look out for each other and we can keep a secret. Imani's secret is that Byron James is her dad. Deke's secret is that he used to be a bully. Lots of secrets. For instance, we applaud and cheer when our new principal hands out a special award in memory of Anthony "Tony" Meeks, who "lost his life trying to help the other survivors."

That may not be the Crazy River truth, but it's our truth. Because of what we chose to tell them, his family believes he died a hero, and that's a good thing, right? Or wrong?

You decide.

Afterword

HOW TO SURVIVE IN THE WILDERNESS

FIRE

The ability to make and maintain a fire can be essential to survival. A fire keeps you warm, boils water, and cooks food. Any vehicle venturing anywhere near a wilderness should carry an emergency kit that includes fire starters. Fire-starter kits are available at most camping or outdoor stores. Most include waterproof matches, self-igniting fire-starter blocks, and ferro rods, which easily produce a shower of very hot sparks. Some ferro rods have a built-in compass, making them doubly useful.

WATER

Water from streams, rivers, or underground sources should be boiled first as a precaution against parasites and pollution.

KNIFE

A folding-blade knife is an indispensable tool. You can cut small branches for a shelter, whittle kindling for the fire, and dig for water with the blade.

SHELTER

If the decision is made to stay in one place and await rescue, building a shelter is a wise thing to do, even if the season is warm. If the weather is cold, a shelter is essential for survival. Shelters can be made from a variety of materials at hand—broken branches, moss, and piles of leaves sandwiched between sticks and branches. Type "how to build a wilderness survival shelter" into a search engine and study the results.

FOOD

Fish, if you can catch it. Crickets, grasshoppers, grubs. Anybody want a toasted worm? Yum! Dandelions and wild asparagus are safe to consume. Best to avoid wild mushrooms and unidentified berries, as some types can be poisonous.

ATTITUDE

Experts suggest that a good attitude—optimistic and energetic, with a can-do spirit—may be the most important key to survival.

INTERESTED IN FURTHER STUDY?

Ask your librarian to recommend books on the subject, or type "how to survive in the wilderness" into a search engine.

Note:

Readers of *Wild River* may have noticed that the kids who

survived did not boil river water before drinking. Why? They had no idea it was a necessary precaution! The fact that the Crazy River water was safe to drink was just pure luck. Rainwater, which they mostly relied on, does not need to be boiled. On the subject of food, it's too bad Deacon Bailey didn't try to find natural food like crickets, grasshoppers, and grubs instead of stealing freeze-dried rations. But that would have been a different story . . .

Acknowledgments

Thanks to my old friend Herbert Barrett for his expertise in the Spanish language.

About the Author

Newbery Honor author Rodman Philbrick grew up on the coast of New Hampshire and has been writing novels since the age of sixteen. Eventually he turned to the genre of adult mystery-and-suspense thrillers and published his first novel at the age of twenty-eight.

Freak the Mighty, Philbrick's first book for young readers, was published by Scholastic. Now considered a classic, it has sold more than five million copies and was made into a movie, *The Mighty*. Philbrick wrote a sequel, *Max the Mighty*, because "so many kids wrote to me suggesting ideas for a sequel that I decided I'd better write one myself before someone else did."

Philbrick's rip-roaring historical novel about an inveterate teller of tall tales, *The Mostly True Adventures of Homer P. Figg*, was set during the Civil War, and was chosen as a 2010 Newbery Honor Book. The Kennedy Center commissioned a theatrical production, which premiered in 2012. Another novel that examines American history is *Zane and the Hurricane: A Katrina Story*, about Zane Dupree and his dog, Bandit, who are trapped in New Orleans just as Hurricane Katrina hits the city. This dramatic survival tale is both heroic and poignant, educating readers about an unforgettable catastrophe.

Wildfire, a 2019 Book Fairs selection, is a thrilling story set in the tinder-dry forests of Maine. *School Library Journal*'s starred review called it "an intense tale of survival and action."

Philbrick engages young readers with stories about ordinary children who are suddenly faced with seemingly insurmountable obstacles—and must summon up courage they don't even know they have. For this ability to connect with readers, Rodman Philbrick's books have been given awards and nominations by more than thirty-five states—often multiple times.

More award-winning novels from Newbery Honor author
RODMAN PHILBRICK